AFTERMATH

A HARRY STARKE NOVEL BOOK 14

BLAIR HOWARD

ISBN-10: 1798483149

ISBN-13: 978-1798483145

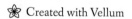

DEDICATION

For Jo, as always

SATURDAY, FEBRUARY 10, 2018

L ewis Walker was tired... No, he was worn out. It was close to midnight, and he'd been driving almost non-stop for close to fourteen hours; he was just about done in. His eyelids felt like lead.

He turned the air conditioner up as high as it would go and, for a moment or two, reveled in the icy blast.

Ridiculous, he thought. *It's friggin' February, for god's sake. I never signed up for this kind of shit.* He looked at the dashboard clock. *Geez, another hour, maybe. Hell. I gotta take a break.*

He reached for his iPhone, looked down at it, selected Maps, and began to tap in a search for the nearest truck stop.

He'd typed in the first three letters when there was a terrific bang on the driver's side, and the truck veered to the right onto the hard shoulder. Out of the corner of his eye, he saw a small black SUV tilted over onto its driver's side wheels, heading at high speed onto the median where it flipped and rolled.

Oh, shit—shit, shit. This ain't happenin'. Walker stamped on the brakes and fought the wheel as the heavily loaded box van slid along the crash barrier and finally came to rest, the diesel engine still running.

He shifted into neutral and glanced at his side mirrors: to the right he could see only the torn metal of the van hard up against the steel barrier. In the left mirror, the road to the rear was clear; he could see nothing on the road in either direction except for the SUV a hundred yards back in the center of the median. It was on its roof and flames were already flickering under the engine compartment.

"SHIT!" he yelled, banging the steering wheel with his fists.

I gotta go see if they're hurt, get them out of there... He pushed open his door and started to exit the truck, hesitated, thinking hard. *I can't. Damn it! What the hell am I gonna do? I gotta get outa here. They catch me with this lot I'm done. Damn. DAMN!*

He pulled the door closed, slammed the gearshift into drive, stomped on the pedal and, with a shriek of tearing, grinding metal, he drove back out onto the road heading east up Monteagle Mountain toward Chattanooga.

A mile or so later, having heard no sirens, he began to breathe a little easier. *I gotta get off this friggin' highway...*

There was a ramp up ahead, just a couple of miles. He slowed the box van, turned right onto the ramp and then right again onto the two-lane highway. Where the hell he was going, he had no idea. One thing he did know was that he had to ditch the truck, but first, he had to take care of his load.

He turned into a roadside pull-in and opened the Maps app on his phone, tapped the screen, swiped it, swiped it again, tapped some more, then smiled. *Got it.*

He took a burner phone from the glove box, tapped in the number and waited.

"Yes. What is it? No names and be quick."

Damn! Friggin' Santy Claus himself. It just had to be him.

He explained the situation, told the voice on the line where he was, where he was going, and the GPS coordinates.

"The cargo, it's intact?"

"Yes."

"Good. The Huey will be there in... forty-five minutes. Stay the hell out of sight until then. Then transfer the cargo and burn the truck. Make sure you leave nothing that can identify you. Understand?" He didn't wait for an answer. He hung up.

Lewis shook his head, exasperated, then grinned. *Okay, asshole.*

And that's how it went, except he had one more thing to do. Lewis removed the chip from the phone and tossed it into the undergrowth at the side of the pull-in. He tossed the phone itself into a creek some two miles on as he drove the box van to the designated location. He parked in what, at some time in the not too distant past, must have been a gravel pit. *Perfect,* he thought. *Couldn't have picked it better.*

He exited the truck, found a comfortable spot under a tree, lit up a smoke and settled down to wait for the helicopter. It arrived right on time. The cargo was duly transferred from the van to the chopper, and the van was set ablaze. Lewis grinned down from the open door. The van was an inferno. What could go wrong?

The TBI, Tennessee Bureau of Investigation, arrested Lewis a week later and charged him with a litany of offenses including two counts of vehicular homicide and leaving the scene of an accident.

2

MAY 22, 2018 – MIDNIGHT

I t was a beautiful evening that twenty-second day of May. It was late, getting on for midnight, and I was driving home from the hospital, on Lookout Mountain's Scenic Highway. The moon was full, the sky a vast field of stars, the city lights below and to the east a glittering blanket of jewels. The great Tennessee River, an immense ribbon of liquid silver, meandered eastward into the distance—past the cooling towers of the Sequoya Nuclear plant that had played such a huge part in my life over the past several days—until it finally disappeared beyond the horizon. It was a spectacular panorama unlike any other on the planet, and I saw none of it... Well, I saw it, but it didn't register; that day in May had been one of the worst of my life.

Thirty minutes earlier I'd been sitting beside Amanda's bed, holding her hand. I was in a state of... Hell, I've no idea. All I knew was that my best friend, my beautiful wife was lying in a coma from which she might never awake. I'd stroked her sweet face and gently kissed her bruised lips.

Her eyelids didn't even flutter.

"Hey," I whispered. "If you can hear me, and I pray to God that you can, I want you to know, I got him. It was Duvon who ran you off the road. I got him. He's dead. It's over."

But I knew deep down it wasn't—Shady would still have to be dealt with, sometime.

"Oh, and there's one more thing, sweetheart: the baby. She's safe and beautiful. The doctors delivered her after the accident. I named her Jade, after the color of your eyes. I hope that's okay."

Again, there was no reaction, nothing. I sat there for a few minutes more, staring at her poor injured face, and then I left. I had to.

AND SO I drove home that night, thinking of the events of the past several days, and that day in particular. On the whole, I was well satisfied with what I'd done. It wouldn't be an overstatement to say that I'd saved the city of Chattanooga from total nuclear destruction. I was a hero, damn it—a reluctant hero for sure—but man, did I ever pay the price for it.

I didn't intend to kill Duvon James, and wouldn't have, but for the Derringer. I'd have turned him over to Kate—that's Kate Gazzara, a cop and my ex-partner—and let the law deal with him.

Then there was Shady, aka Lester Tree, bad guy

extraordinaire, and my nemesis. He was gone, for now at least, into the Federal Witness Protection Program, but I knew he'd never forget, or quit, and that meant that sooner or later I had to confront him. When, how, where? Who the hell knew? I didn't: it was something I'd have to figure out another day. For now, I had a child to look after and...my wife.

I ARRIVED at my home on East Brow Road atop Lookout Mountain at a little after midnight. The house was dark, cold, bleak, as was my mood. *If I lose Amanda... Goddammit.* I shuddered at the thought. *I suppose I should call my father... Nope, can't. Can't think... Jade? Later, tomorrow. Can't do it today... I don't think I could handle it. Right now, I need a frickin' drink.*

I poured myself what had to be a half-pint of Laphroaig in a tumbler and topped it off with ice cubes, grabbed the now half-empty bottle by the neck, then stepped out onto the patio.

I placed the bottle on a table beside a lounger and sat down. I cradled the brimming glass in both hands, put it to my lips and... sucked. The level of the liquid in the tumbler dropped by a third. I swallowed—no, I gulped— almost choked as more than three ounces of the fiery liquid hit the back of my throat and seared my gullet on its way south and into my bloodstream.

I coughed, coughed again, and again, then took a deep breath, wiped my eyes, closed them and lay back, the heavy glass still in my hands. Ten minutes later, it was empty, and I refilled it. My head should already have been swimming, and that was just where I wanted to be. I wanted to forget, but I couldn't: my head remained clear...and so did the memories and, Amanda... *Why? Why did she do it? I told her to... to; dammit, I told her to take the back road...*

I closed my eyes, shook my head, sat up, stood, stepped across the patio, skirting the edge of the pool, to the wall, sat down on it, and stared unseeing into the distance. The moon had moved on, westward. The river had darkened, but the lights of the city were still spectacular, but I only know that because they always are.

I must have sat there for an hour or more before I finally rose and went back to the lounger, my glass long-since empty, but I didn't refill it; I couldn't, the damned bottle was empty. I could have fetched more from the house, but I couldn't be bothered and besides, I wasn't enjoying it. The funny thing was though, I'd just swilled down a fifth of single malt scotch and didn't even have a buzz on.

So, I lay back and closed my eyes, thinking, remembering...mostly about my wife, Amanda, and the past three years. But also the events of the past five weeks that led up to that night, that moment...images of the bomb, tumbling downward, end over end into the water, the explosion, the waterspout, the faces of the people that had died during the hunt for the bomb... And, later that evening, Duvon's body, twisting and turning in the air as it tumbled from the aircraft into the same lake I'd dropped the bomb. *Yeah, finally that son of a bitch was going to meet his maker, and it was downhill all the way.*

Welcome to the gates of Hell, Duvon... But the one image I couldn't get out of my head was that of Amanda lying there, silent, pale, unresponsive...

It was at that point I must have fallen asleep, because the next thing I knew, someone was shaking my arm.

"Harry... *Harry,* wake up."

~

W*HAT THE HELL?* *Ooowuh, oh shit, my head is coming apart. Oh, dear God...*

I guess that fifth of Laphroaig hit me harder than I thought. I had a splitting headache... No, my head felt like that damn bomb had exploded inside it. I struggled to sit up, tried to hide my eyes from the sun with one hand and push myself upright with the other.

"*Kate?*" I said, shading my eyes, looking up at her, trying to bring her face into focus. "What the hell are you doing here? What time is it? Geez, I need a drink."

"It's almost eleven. Jacque called me. She's been trying to reach you. You're not answering your phone or texts. God, what a mess you are. You need a drink? The hell you do. Looks like you had more than enough last night."

"*Naw.* Hell, no. Not that. Coffee, I need coffee... Eleven o'clock in the morning? Damn. That's never happened to me before."

She stood over me like a damned statue, a beautiful statue, feet apart, hands on hips, face serious, eyes staring down at me. *Oh shit, is she ever pissed.*

I stood, staggered sideways, a little. She put out a

hand to steady me. I waved it away, took a half-step forward, and again I almost went down. This time I allowed her to help.

She steered me into the house, the bedroom, pushed me down onto the bed, knelt down and grabbed my shoe.

"You need a shower in the worst way, Harry."

"Hey, *hey*," I said, gently pushing her away. "Don't do that. I can do it. Go make some coffee...*please?*"

And she did.

Twenty minutes later I was showered, dressed comfortably in jeans and a tee and feeling half-human again and heading for the kitchen and, I hoped, a half-gallon of Dark Italian Roast. Bless her, Kate had outdone herself. Not only was there a full carafe of the good stuff waiting but also breakfast in the form of a monster chopped egg sandwich. *How the hell did she do that? I looked last night: no bread in the house.*

She must have read my mind. "I found it in the freezer. Thank God for the microwave. Eat. You'll feel better."

"I already feel better," I said, grabbing a pint coffee mug from the cupboard. "Coffee is what I need. The sandwich is a bonus. Thanks."

"So sit," she said. "Talk to me."

"Oh shit, Kate," I said, sitting down at the table. "About what?"

"About what the hell happened to you last night... No, I don't want to know how you pulled it off, but the national press does. They are at your office and right outside, on Brow Road. They want to interview you, Harry. You're a hero."

"The hell I am... Oh wow, that hurts." I put my hand to my aching head. "I can't do it, Kate. I just can't. Get rid of 'em, will you?"

"Hah, you've got to be kidding. They're not going away, *ev-er!*"

"Then you've got to get me the hell out of here. I've got to go to Amanda...and I haven't talked to Dad...and I need to see Jade—"

"Jade? Who the hell? Oh, I see. The baby. Of course. Whew."

She thought for a minute, then said, "Where is she?"

"Jade? With August and Rose, at their house."

"Okay. So I already checked on Amanda. There's no change... Oh, Harry, I'm so sorry, but no change is not bad, right?"

I glared across the table at her.

"I know, I know, but she's hanging in there, and she will. She's tough. You're right, though, you need to get out of here, and you can't go to the hospital. They'll find you there. So, we go to August. His property is gated—"

"Uh, yeah. So's this one, but the press is here anyway."

"How are you on your feet? Can you walk?"

"Oh, for God's sake, Kate. I only had a couple of drinks—" I caught the look. It wasn't pleasant. "Yeah, I can walk just fine...but I dunno. I can't get her out of my head. The way...she is."

"I know, and I understand, but you have to pull your-self together. If not for Amanda, for the baby. Get a frickin' grip, Harry. This is not like you."

I stared at her; she stared back, defiantly, waiting.

I broke first, something that never would have happened if...

"Okay," I said. "You win. What's the plan?"

"You're not going to like it."

"Tell me."

And she did, and she was right. I didn't like it.

There are three rear doors to my house. Two of them —the patio door in the living room and the kitchen door that also provides access to the patio—could be seen by anyone looking over the perimeter wall on East Brow. The third door is in the basement, in my office. It opens onto a much smaller, lower patio and the trees and shrubland on the mountainside, and it can't be seen, from anywhere. Unfortunately, the terrain is steep, rocky, and densely forested.

From that basement door to Scenic Highway below is about seven hundred feet, almost straight down through the forest, and that's what she wanted me to do; hike down the damned mountain. But that wasn't all. I then had to hike north another five or six hundred feet to a pull-off on the highway where she'd pick me up. *In my condition? Are you freaking kidding me?*

"I guess I'd better put on another shirt," I said. "It's pretty wild country out there." *Geez, is that ever an understatement?*

Despite the heat outside—it was in the eighties—I also donned a heavy leather jacket which I hoped would provide some protection from the blackthorn and brambles and such, and ten minutes later I was heading out the door and down the mountain.

Fifty minutes later—yeah, it took that long—I scrambled into the passenger side of her unmarked cruiser. I was exhausted, filthy from head to toe, and so thirsty I could have emptied that freakin' lake I dropped the bomb into.

Holy shit! That's it. I've had enough. I can't do this anymore. I'm done, this time for good. I gotta get away.

Yes, I was in a pretty black mood, but things were about to change, and not for the better.

3

MAY 23, 2018 – NOON

W e rode the rest of the way down the mountain in silence. Not because I wasn't in the mood for conversation or because I had nothing to say. The enormity of the events of the past several weeks was overwhelming, hard to grasp.

The tires of the big car squealed as she negotiated the tight bend at the foot of the mountain, jerking me out of my reverie as she merged smoothly into the traffic on Lee Highway.

I don't recall exactly what I was thinking, but I do remember asking her what the plan was.

"Riverview! Your dad's place, you said."

I glanced at her, shook my head, then said, "No, I don't think so. Not right now. I need to talk to Jacque and Bob first."

She didn't look at me, but I saw the muscles of her jaw tighten. "I don't know how you think we can pull that off," she said. "The press are all over Georgia Avenue for several blocks. We had to send traffic units. It's a mess."

I thought for a minute. "Okay, Riverview it is. I'll have them come there."

I slipped my phone out of my pocket and pushed the speed dial for Jacque Hale, my business partner and personal assistant.

"Hey..."

"Oh m'god," she almost shouted. "Where d'hell are you? We bin outa our minds wid worry."

Black as my mood was, I couldn't help but smile. Jacque is Jamaican, but she'd lost her accent sometime back when she was in school except, that is, when she gets excited, and boy was she excited.

"I went home... Look, we need to talk. I'm on my way to August's house. You and Bob come on over soon as you can. Okay?"

"But—"

"No buts. Quit whatever you're doing and get over there. I'll be waiting." I disconnected before she could answer.

August and Rose were in the sitting room; Jade, my daughter, was in a bassinet in their bedroom, my first stop after I said hello... No, it wasn't quite that simple. Rose, tears streaming down her cheeks, grabbed hold of me and wouldn't let go. When she did finally turn me loose, August took a step forward and offered me his hand. I shook my head and grinned, my father never was one to show his emotions, and that day he was no different except... well, he seemed a little more distant than usual. I thought little of it, though; I was too wrapped up in myself, but I did take his hand and shake it.

"Well done, son," he said, looking me right in the eye. "I'm proud of you."

I nodded, let go of his hand and grabbed him, pulled him in close, and whispered in his ear, "Thanks, you old goat. I love you too." I felt him nod, slightly, and I smiled and turned him loose.

I left Kate with August. Rose went to make hot tea, and I went to see my daughter. She was asleep, and I didn't have the heart to wake her, so I simply sat on the edge of the bed and watched her, my brain a maelstrom of disconnected thoughts and emotions. I must have sat there thinking about life—mine, Amanda's, Jade's—and the future and what it might hold until Rose knocked gently on the open door and informed me that everyone was there.

I nodded, absently, and she left me alone again. I took a couple of minutes more, then stood, leaned over the bassinet, and kissed my daughter gently on the forehead. She stirred in her sleep, threw up her arms, tiny fists up and ready for a fight. I smiled, *Just like your stupid father... Yeah, but no more.*

They were all scattered around the great room, seated, holding or sipping cups of hot tea, staring up at me.

"What?" I asked, but before anyone could answer, I shook my head. "No, don't go there. I'm not in the mood. Read about it in the papers for god's sake or watch TV. They *always* get it right."

"So why are we here?" Bob asked.

Bob Ryan is my other business partner. He's also my lead investigator. He's worked for me almost since day one, when I first opened the agency. Now he's a twenty-five percent shareholder in the company. Jacque also has twenty-five percent. Bob's a year older than I am, a big man, six feet two and 240 pounds of solid muscle with a wry sense of humor. He, like me, is also an ex-cop—Chicago PD. He's also an ex-marine... At least, I thought he was. He's a quiet man, dedicated, but deadly: not someone you want to screw around with.

"As I told Jacque," I began, "we need to talk." I paused, looking at each of them. They waited. I shook my head and said, "I'm not coming back."

"What?" Jacque asked, her brow furrowed. "I'm not understandin'."

I started pacing. "It's simple enough. I'm not coming back. I quit. It's all yours, yours and Bob's. Run with it."

"Harry," August said, "this is not the time for this kind of thinking. You're upset, and rightly so, but you *must* give it some time. Don't fly off the handle and do something you'll regret."

I looked at him, shook my head, smiled at him, then said, "Regret? You say *regret*? Hah! I already have way too many of those. If only... No, Dad. This is something I should have done a long time ago... If I had—well, I didn't, so we won't go there. Look, it was never supposed to be like this... this... Do you have any idea what I—" I looked at Bob, shook my head, and said, "Sorry, Bob, what we just went through? I, that is we, killed almost a dozen men these last couple of days. I dumped Duvon James' body into that radioactive cauldron, for god's sake. Who does stuff like that? Come *on, tell me.* No comment? Then I'll tell you: Nobody... No-body!"

I looked at Kate, then at my father, and then continued, "When I left the PD, I thought I had it made: a nice easy life doing what I do best, what I love, investigations. I had a good book of business: attorneys, corporate clients, banks, and that's what I wanted, what I thought it was going to be all about, and for a while it was."

I looked at Kate and continued. "Then here you come, Kate," I said, bitterly.

She looked stunned, opened her mouth to speak, but I held up my hand.

"No, don't say anything. You—okay, you and the chief—dragged me into one impossible criminal case after another. That was *not* what I wanted, but even that would have been okay, except that people started getting hurt, my people... Remember Calaway Jones, Kate? I almost died, remember? That never would have happened if you hadn't...sent me after Harper. And that's when I ran into Lester Tree, again, which wouldn't have been so bad except for the fact that I ruined his entire operation, and the SOB has dogged me ever since. Now I'm to spend the rest of my days looking over my shoulder, waiting for him to appear, and one day he will."

I paused, took a breath and said, "Then, Kate, when I needed you, you turned your back on me. Yeah, I'm talking about Jim Wallace. Well, no more. I'm done with it. Right now, all I can think about is Amanda...and Jade, and what's going to happen to them. I swear to God... Well, I'll never put either of them through anything like this again."

"Harry," Bob said, his elbows on his knees, hands cradling his glass, looking up at me. "We don't want it.

Not without you. It's your company. Without you, there is no company, not one I want a part of anyway. So please, take some time, think it over. It will get better. It always does. And don't worry about Tree. I'll take care of him."

I had to smile, just a little, at that. Bob's always had my back... Yeah, he's killed for me. And I had no doubt he'd do it again. Only I wasn't about to let him, but I nodded anyway.

"Harry." The voice was soft, gentle. It was Rose. "You can't do this. You have a dozen people working for you, relying on you for their livelihood. Tim, think about Tim. He loves you, Harry. He's a puppy. He couldn't function without you." She looked at Jacquie, shook her head, looked down at the carpet, silent.

"Rose's right, Harry," August said. "You have responsibilities. You can't just quit."

I opened my mouth to speak, but he raised a hand, stopped me, and continued.

"And, for the record," he said, looking first at Kate, then at me, "none of the events of the past several years are Kate's fault. You made your own damn choices, now live with them. What you're contemplating is weak. I can't believe you're even considering it. I—" He paused, stared at me across the table. "Do you have any idea what life would have been like if you hadn't done what you did? Today, right now, Hamilton County would be a radioactive wasteland. Yes, I understand how you feel, to some extent, but to throw up your hands and quit?" He shook his head, stood, looked at me for a long moment, then turned away and left the room.

Ah, for god's sake...

I followed him to the door. "Okay, Dad, I get it. Come on back. I'll... I'll think about it." *I'll think about it. Yeah, and that's all I'll do.*

At the time, I meant what I said: I was done with it, and there was nothing anyone could say or do to make me change my mind. But life, cruel mistress that she is, has a way of sideswiping me, always has, and that time it took her less than ten minutes to turn me upside down.

I looked around at the rest of the group. They were all staring at me.

"What?" I asked, angrily.

No one spoke. Jacque's face had drained of its color. Bob was slowly shaking his head, his lips clamped together. Rose... her face a mask, held my gaze then turned her head away. Only Kate seemed unperturbed by it all. I waited several minutes, hoping August would return; he didn't.

That's not like him...

"Okay, Rose," I said. "Something's happened. What is it? What's going on?"

She turned and looked at me. "It's not for me to say," she said, quietly. "I think you should ask your father."

There was something about the look she was giving me. I nodded. "Okay, I will." And I did.

I found him in his study... Hmm, I should tell you about my dad.

My father, August Starke, is a lawyer, one of the best in the country. He specializes in tort, which is an upmarket way of saying "personal injury." His ads run on most local stations almost every day; and that damn jingle, geez, it embarrasses the hell out of me. My father is a showman, wealthy almost beyond comprehension. He's a billionaire.

He's sixty-eight years old and cuts an imposing figure. He's an inch taller than me, silver-haired, lean, toned, works out every other morning, is sickeningly healthy, and carries not a pound of extra fat. He's also the most competitive man I've ever met. He's a tiger in the courtroom and on the golf course. He gets more pleasure out of winning ten bucks on the greens than he does in winning a multi-million-dollar class action. August Starke is an enigma, even to me.

He has a brain like a computer and is the only man I know that can carry two trains of thought at the same time, an ability that had served him well, in his personal and private life.

He's been married twice; first to my mother, and now to Rose... Rose is also an enigma. She's twenty years younger than August, just three years older than me. She's a very beautiful woman: tall, blond, perfect skin, perfect figure. To those who don't know her well, she's the quintessential "trophy wife," but that's not her at all. In reality, she's a very caring individual and loves my old man dearly. I, in turn, love her for it.

Anyway, as I said, I found him in his study. He was standing at the window overlooking the sixth fairway. I stepped over to the window and stood beside him. He didn't turn his head.

"I suppose Rose told you, then?" he said.

"She told me nothing. Talk to me August."

For a moment he didn't speak. Neither did I. I simply waited.

"It's Joseph," he said, quietly. "He's gone."

"What do you mean, he's gone? He's dead?"

Joseph, Uncle Joe, is my father's younger brother, and he's... Oh hell, he's what they call a "special needs" person. His mental capacity is that of a seven-year-old. No, he wasn't born like that. At six months he developed an infection and the doctor gave him penicillin. Unfortunately, he was allergic to it and it fried his brain. Today, he's fifty-six and lives in a facility that caters to his needs.

"Not dead," August said. "Abducted. Someone picked him up at the nursing home two days ago and didn't return him. He's missing."

I was stunned. I stared at him. He continued to gaze out of the window.

"How the hell did they get him out, and why didn't you tell me?" I asked.

He turned and looked at me, a slight smile on his lips. "Why didn't I tell you? How was I supposed to do that? You've been rather busy."

Yeah, my old man could do sarcasm. It served him well in court, but it washed over me.

Anyway, he was right, and I didn't say anything. I just nodded, and he turned again to stare out the window.

"He said he was you," August said, quietly.

"What? What are you talking about?"

"You asked how someone got him out. The man who picked him up said he was you."

"You're kidding, right?"

He shook his head.

"So, he was kidnapped. That's what you're telling me. Have you told the police?"

He gave me a withering look. "What do you think? Of course I have, but with what's been going on these last few days—"

"Do you have any idea why...or who?"

"No."

"And the kidnapper has not been in touch?"

Again, he gifted me with a sarcastic look, but he said nothing.

I put a hand on his shoulder. "Okay, Dad. I'm on it, with everything I have. I'll find him, I promise. Let's go back and talk to the others." And that's what we did.

4

MAY 23, 2018 1PM

"Kate," I said glaring at her as I reentered the living room, followed by my father. "Did you know about this? Because if you did—"

"Know about what?" she interrupted me.

"She didn't," August said. "No one but Rose knows."

"But you said you'd informed the pol—"

"And I did." Now it was August that interrupted me. "And I also told you that they had more to worry about than a missing mental patient."

Geez, he's never called him that before.

"Joe?" Kate asked. "Joe's missing? How? What happened?"

"Someone purporting to be Harry checked him out of the facility two days ago," August said. "We've heard nothing of him since."

"Harry?" Kate asked. "The person who took him said he was Harry?"

"That's right," August said.

"I don't get it," she said, shaking her head. "Why Harry?"

"I asked myself the same question," I said, sitting down next to Jacque. "I don't know."

"Just one person, right?" Bob asked as he flipped through the screens on his phone. "Okay. Do you have a description of the man?"

"Yes, I have a description," August said, "for what it's worth. Tall, medium build, in his early forties with either dark or light brown hair... Oh, and he was wearing glasses. That's it."

"Signature?" Bob asked.

"Harry Starke."

"And no ransom demand, at least not yet?" Bob said.

"No, and it's been two days," I said. "If they were after money, we'd have heard by now, so it's personal. Whoever took him has a grudge, either against me or maybe even you, August. If it's me—"

"How about Shady?" Jacque asked.

I shook my head. "No, two days ago he was already in custody." I thought for a minute. "There are plenty of people I can think of that might have reason to go after me, but I can't think of a one that would take Joe. Not many people know about him... He has no family other than you and me, Dad. What cases are you working? Can you think of anything, anyone?"

August thought for a minute, then shook his head and said, "Nothing sensitive: three class action suits that have been running for almost three years, two against big pharma—birth control and one for mesothelioma. Between them, I'm representing more than seven hundred clients... Aside from those, I have several local corporate clients, and I took on a wrongful death suit for Jack Martin, whom I think you know. That's about it. Nothing of any importance, other than those."

I did know Jack. He was a member of the country club. He wasn't exactly a friend of mine, but he was one of August's inner circle. I'd played golf with him on several occasions. I liked him well enough.

"What bothers me most," I said, "is that we've heard nothing from the people who took him."

"Not yet, we haven't," Bob said, "but we will. It's either a straight ransom for money or it's personal... payback, maybe. I'd say we'll know very shortly. Whoever has him won't want to be saddled with a... Well, you know what I mean."

I did know what he meant, and so did everyone else in the room. We all knew what he was implying. It had been more than forty-eight hours since they took him: poor old Joe, bless him, was as good as dead.

Kate nodded, then said, "It's already been too long. We need to move, and quickly. How do you want to proceed, Harry?"

"We start at the nursing home. They'll have security cameras, right?" I asked.

"I would imagine that they do," August said.

"I'm on it," Bob said as he stood.

"No," I said. "Wait. I'll come with you. August, this doesn't sound like Big Pharma. So if this has nothing to do with the class action suits, could it be the wrongful death suit?"

He thought for a moment, then shook his head. "It

could, I suppose," August said, "but I doubt it. Although..."

"Talk to me, August," I said. "Who and what are you dealing with?"

"I'm suing a company in Atlanta. Christmas Security Concepts, known as CSC. It's a private security agency."

At the mention of the name, Bob turned and looked at him, his eyes narrowed. *He knows them. Good.*

"So what happened?" I asked.

"Three months ago, on an evening in February, Jack Martin's mother and father were returning home from Nashville when they were run off the road by a truck. The driver of the truck, Lewis Walker, left the scene, just left them there to die. They burned to death. The truck, a Ford E350 box van, turned out to be stolen. Walker dumped it in an abandoned gravel pit on top of the mountain and torched it. Walker works for CSC. I'm suing the company with Walker as a codefendant. That's it. It's not complicated."

"What do we know about Walker?" Bob asked. "And if he burned the truck, how did they catch him? At the scene, or what?"

"Not at the scene. They might not have caught him at all, but he made a mistake. The sheriff called in the TBI —Tennessee Bureau of Investigation. They processed the scene. They figured someone must have picked him up, and that he had to wait because they found two cigarette butts under a tree some fifty yards from the burned-out van. Walker, it turns out, is ex-military. His DNA is on record."

"Well, that's a break," I said. "We'll need to talk to him."

"Why?" Jacque asked. "We don't yet know if the case has anything to do with Joe's abduction."

"You're right, Jacque, we don't, but it's the only lead we have, so that's where we'll start... Okay, I need you to get with Tim and have him research CSC and Walker. I want everything, and I mean everything, he can find."

I looked at Kate. "How about you? You in?"

She gave me a look that would have frozen a waterfall. "You sure you want me?"

I sighed. "You know I do. I didn't mean any of that crap, and I'm sorry. I was just venting. So, are you in?"

"Of course you meant it, but yes. It's Joe. What do you want me to do?"

"Find out where Lewis Walker is being held. If he's at the sheriff's department, we're screwed."

"He's not," August said. "He made bail. He's been out almost three months."

"You're kidding," Kate said. "Two counts of vehicular homicide? How much was his bail?"

"His attorney, Ham Cronin, was able to get it down to half-a-million," August said. "CSC stood surety for it. He was out the same day and gone the next."

"Cronin? Hamilton Cronin from Atlanta?" I asked, already knowing the answer.

"That's the one."

"Geez, he has one hell of a reputation," I said, shaking my head, "and it's not good. From what I've heard, he's a rare piece of work, almost as crooked as the clients he represents."

"And Walker skipped?" Kate asked.

August nodded.

"So, CSC is out a half-million in bail money," I said, more to myself than to anyone else. "That's interesting. I wonder if it was part of their plan. Sounds like a write-off to me, to get him out of the way. How's the case going, August?"

"They're denying any liability, claiming Walker was acting alone. Unfortunately, now he's gone so we can't question him."

"You say he wasn't acting alone," I said. "How do you know?"

"He couldn't have been. There's no doubt he was driving the van that he torched. His DNA puts him at the scene, so someone must have picked him up. But it's not just that. It had been raining earlier that evening, and there was only one set of tire tracks into the gravel pit; those belonged to the van. Secondly, the TBI determined that the van was carrying a load when it went into the pit —they figured that out from the depth of the tire tracks— but the burned-out carcass was empty. There was no sign of the load, and no other tracks in or out, which means..." He paused and shook his head. "Which makes one wonder how they got Walker and the cargo out of there... They think it could only have been done by a helicopter. I'd say he's long gone, out of the country."

"Maybe, but we need to find him. Jacque, that's another job for Tim. Have him get on it right away."

She nodded and jotted in her notebook.

"Kate, this is officially a missing persons case. Can you get it assigned to you?"

She nodded. "I'll talk to the chief, and Carpenter. She won't like it, but it shouldn't be a problem."

"Carpenter?" I asked.

"Lieutenant Judy Carpenter. Missing Persons is her department."

I nodded, then said, "So, unless we hear from the kidnappers, we don't have much to work with. But as we all know, time is of the essence in cases like this, so we have to do what we can with what we have. Right now, until we find out differently, that's Walker and CSC." I paused to see if there were any more questions.

"Okay, everyone," I said, rising to my feet. "Let's get to it. Kate, I'll talk to you later. Jacque, call me as soon as you have something. Bob, you're with me. Dad, I can't go to the office, so I need a place where I can work, and I need access to a computer."

"You can use my office, and you can stay here for as long as you like. You can have one of the guest rooms. Rose?"

She nodded. "He can have the suite. I'll see that it's prepared."

"Thank you, Rose," I said. "Bob, let's talk."

I took Bob back to my father's office, closed the door and we sat down; me at the computer, Bob in an easy chair by the window.

I searched the internet for CSC.

"Hah," I said, "it's just as I figured, Bob. CSC is a private military company headquartered in Atlanta, Georgia, founded by Nicholas Christmas in March 2009. It seems that Nick is running his own little private army."

"That's right. He is."

"You know this Nicholas Christmas then?"

"Oh yes, I know him," Bob said. "I had several dealings with him when I was in Afghanistan. He's a piece of work, smart but about as crooked as you'll find. I couldn't prove it at the time, but I knew he was dealing drugs, and I'm betting that's what was in that van—"

"Wait," I interrupted him. "*You* couldn't prove it? What does that mean? You were a Marine..." I caught the look in his eyes and paused, then I got it. "You were *not* a Marine?"

He grinned at me but said nothing.

"I had Tim do extensive background checks on you. You were a Marine. You served for twelve years. You were a captain..." I let it die, watching his face. He was still smiling.

"What? All these years you've led me to believe... Just what the hell were you then?" I asked, shaking my head, dumbfounded.

"You know what they say," he said, laughing. "I could tell you, but then I'd have to kill you."

"Oh, for Pete's sake. Get over yourself. What the hell were you doing all those years?"

Now he was serious. "I can't tell you, Harry. What I did is covered by the Espionage Act."

"So, you weren't a Marine, then you must have... You were either NSA or CIA." And there it was, that telltale twitch of his left eye. "Holy Mary, you were CIA."

The smile was gone. He didn't answer. He simply shrugged.

I nodded, grimly, and said, quietly, "I don't give a crap for the Espionage Act. I want to know everything you know about Christmas and his operation. I need to know because if he had anything to do with Joe's disappearance, I have to go after him. You know that."

He nodded. "I do, but you can't. The man is running a private army for god's sake. You can't go up against that."

I stared at him, unblinking.

He sighed. "Okay, so you can't, but you will." He shook his head and then continued. "Nick Christmas was an Army Ranger, one of the best... Harry, the Navy

SEALs are the glamor boys of the Special Forces. The Rangers get very little press and no glory. They are equally as well-trained as the SEALs, in some cases even better. Christmas is one of those cases. Between 2004 and 2008, he and his team—there were six of them—did three tours in Afghanistan, all of them in Helmand Province.

"It was during those three tours that I got to know him. He was part of MICO, the Rangers Military Intelligence Company. I was—" He shook his head and continued. "He and his team were highly trained Army Rangers operating independently as forward observers in the vicinity of Lashkar Gah, the capital of Helmand Province. This was just before the Afghan presidential elections, and before the Marines launched Operation Khanjar. His job was to provide us with actionable intel. And he was damn good at it, mainly because sometime in 2005, he had the great good fortune to make contact with a minor Afghan warlord known only by the code name Lazarus, a name given to him by Christmas himself. He never revealed his real name."

I grabbed a couple of water bottles out of the small refrigerator in August's office, handed one to Bob, kept the other for myself, and nodded for him to continue.

"So, over a period of almost three years, Christmas was able to build a mutually beneficial relationship between himself and Lazarus. During that period, Lazarus provided Christmas with a great deal of excellent intel, for which he was well-paid. What we didn't know was that it was a two-way street: Nick was supplying Lazarus with information that gave him an

edge over his rivals and kept him safe from us and the
Afghan Security Force. Nick was, in fact, playing for
both sides. His team became our number one source, and
as such he was allowed to do pretty much as he pleased,
just so long as kept on delivering. And he did, right up
until he was discharged. I know because I was directly
involved in analyzing and disseminating his intel."

He paused, thought for a moment, then continued.

"What we didn't know at the time was that
Christmas was also buying heroin from Lazarus, and he
and his buddy, Sergeant Johnson were smuggling it back
into the United States and selling it to a distributor in
Atlanta. At first, the quantities were quite small, but
Nick reinvested the proceeds. By the time he received his
discharge, he'd made a pile of money. He used that
money to start his company, his own private army. As I
said, I could never prove any of that, but I knew."

I sat back in my father's leather chair, unable to
believe what I was hearing. The man had been with me
almost from the beginning. I trusted him, treated him like
a brother. I'd even handed him twenty-five percent of my
company.

"You know what, Bob?" I said. "You're really something. You sit there telling me all this..." I shook my head.
"You came to me in 2008 with a documented employ-
ment history. It was a total fabrication, a lie."

"Not a lie, exactly, more a necessary fabrication."

"Was any of it true?"

He didn't answer. *A necessary fabrication? What the
hell does that mean?*

And then it hit me, and I couldn't believe it.

"No! *No!* You son of a bitch. You're still working for them, the CIA!"

He looked away, then back at me. "In a way, yeah. I'm still on the rolls, not active, but yeah."

I stared at him, my stomach churning. I felt like I was about to throw up.

"All these years," I said, bitterly, "you've been lying to me, Bob. Geez, I always knew you were a piece of work. Always thought you were a borderline sociopath, but now I can understand why it's so easy for you to kill. Bob, never...*never* did I think you'd betray me."

"Damn it, Harry," he said, angrily. "Back the hell off. Do you think I had a choice? I didn't. I haven't betrayed you. I worked every hour you paid me for, and I've always had your back, and I always will. I tried to quit. Yeah, I freakin' did, but they wouldn't let me. I had to take what they offered. Yeah, they can call me back whenever they want, but they haven't, not yet. They've left me the hell alone. And besides, I was able to stay in touch with my contacts...and friends, which has worked damn well for you in the past. Get over it, Harry, or fire me. Whichever suits you." And with that, he stood and turned to leave.

"Sit the hell back down, Bob."

He took another step toward the door, then turned and glared at me across the desk.

"Sit down," I said, quietly.

He sat, then said, "Don't ask. I've already told you more than I should."

"I have to. I need to know what I'm up against."

He glared at me, then seemed to relax a little and said, "What we're up against."

I nodded. "Yeah, that. What we're up against. How well do you know him?"

"Christmas? I don't think anybody really knows him. I met him—oh, I don't know—probably a couple of dozen times. I've been in the field with him and his team twice. He's tough... You don't get to be a captain in the Rangers unless you are. On the surface, he's likable, sort of, for a sociopath." He paused, looked at me wryly, then continued. "Charming, I suppose would be a better word. I got along with him well enough." He stared at the desktop, then looked up at me. "He's a killer, Harry, a stone-cold killer."

"Kinda like you," I said, without humor.

"Screw you, Harry."

I didn't answer. I just stared across the desk at him and waited. Then he said, "I know that he's a killer because I've seen him in action. I spent three days in the mountains north of Gereshk with him and his team. We ran into an ambush. It wasn't a big thing; there couldn't have been more than a dozen of them. Nick deployed his men, and they quickly mopped them up. It was all over in less than fifteen minutes... Yeah, they're that good. Unfortunately, the Taliban left three wounded fighters behind. Our boy Nick popped all three, one after the other, quick as he could pull the trigger. If I'd known what he was about, I would have stopped him, but it happened too quickly." He looked down at the desk for a moment with a frown on his face.

"The bastard enjoyed it," he continued. "I could tell. And I know that wasn't the first time, or the last. I asked him, 'What the hell did you do that for?' He just smiled—

no, not smiled—he laughed, and said, 'the only good Afghan is...' well, you know."

He looked at me, seriously. "So, Harry. Where do we go from here, now that you know what I am?"

Yeah, where the hell do we go from here? I thought. I don't know if I'll ever trust you again. Ten friggin' years you've been lying to me... I don't know. What would Amanda say? She'd... I can't even think about her right now. Get a fricking grip, Harry.

I shook my head, trying to rid myself of...what? I had no idea. My brain felt like it was full of concrete. Then I made up my mind.

I looked at him and said, "I have an uncle to find. Are you in? If so, the past is the past. It always was." But even as I said it, I had a hard time believing it.

He nodded. "Good enough. Yeah, I'm in. You know that. You have a plan?"

"It's coming together," I said, thoughtfully. "Your knowing Christmas might work for us. In the meantime, let's go see if the Sisters of Grace have some video footage we can look at."

6

MAY 23, 2018 5PM

Sisters of Grace
        Located in a somewhat remote area of Hixson northeast of Highway 153, Sisters of Grace was a small Benedictine convent, and they ran one of the oldest and well-thought of nursing homes in the area. Joe had been living there for most of his adult life. As I said, he was a happy person, living in a small world all his own where everyone he met was his friend. He loved to paint, and he was good at it. I have one of his pieces hanging in my office.

Bob and I didn't talk much on the ride over to Sisters that day. What little conversation we did have was strained. Yep, it was going to take some getting used to, knowing that Bob was CIA, active or not, but I'd get there. Anyway, I spent most of the trip remembering the times—and there had been plenty of them—when Bob had saved my ass, and Kate's, and it was only a couple of years ago when he'd saved Amanda's life, at the cost of a bullet to his own shoulder.

It was almost five in the afternoon when we arrived, and as I pulled in through the gates, I glanced sideways at him. He was sitting like a damn statue, upright, stiff, obviously feeling uncomfortable.

"Hey," I said, as I parked the car and turned off the engine. "I think I may owe you an—"

"You owe me nothing, Harry. I'm the one at fault, and I'm sorry for it. But know this: if I could have done things differently, I would have. So—"

I nodded, grabbed his arm and squeezed it. "Forget it, buddy. You've been there for me and mine; you always have. As far as I'm concerned, it's forgotten. Let's do this, okay?"

Forgotten? Not hardly. That was going to take a while, if ever. CIA? Sheesh!

"Geez, Harry, you're one hard-to-read son of a bitch. If I didn't know better, I'd say you were some kind of—"

Whatever he was about to say, he didn't. Instead, he said, "Yeah, let's do it."

I was quite familiar with the Sisters complex. I'd visited Joe, not often, but several times over the years. It had been a while since the last time. *A while? It's been almost a year.*

The business office was just beyond the main entrance, in the Narthex, what I would have normally called the lobby. I tapped on the sliding glass window and was rewarded with a bright smile from a young lady seated at a desk on the far side of the office. She stood and came to the window, slid it open.

"Good afternoon. I'm Sister Victoria. How can I help you?" The soft voice had a slight Irish lilt. The smile was infectious; she was beautiful. *Sister? I thought they all wore those coverings on their head... those habits.*

"My name is Harry Starke. I'm a private inv—"

Her face fell. "Oh my," she interrupted me. "You must be here about Joseph. I'm so sorry, Mr. Starke. Let me get someone who can help you."

She picked up the desk phone, dialed a two-digit number, and waited, the handset to her ear, looking at me.

"Sister, it's Vicky. I have Mr. Harry Starke and one of his associates here. Can you come? Thank you. I'll tell him."

She returned to the window and said, "Sister Julia, our administrator, will be with you shortly. If you'd like to take a seat..." She gestured through the glass at a wooden bench set against the far wall. We sat. I felt like a schoolboy waiting to see the principal. Fortunately, we didn't have to wait long.

Sister Julia was not what I was expecting.

She seemed to appear out of nowhere. I don't know exactly what I expected, but it certainly wasn't what would have passed for a corporate CEO. She was wearing a modest, light gray business suit over a white blouse that was buttoned almost to her chin. The skirt was cut just below the knee. She wore her hair tied back in a bun. The only giveaway that she was a member of the order was the large wooden cross that hung around her neck almost to her waist.

"Mr. Starke," she said, holding out her hand, as she walked quickly toward us. "I'm Sister Mary Julia, you can call me Sister Julia. It's easier and less confusing. We're all named Mary here."

We stood and I shook her hand. Her grip was gentle but firm. I introduced Bob.

"I'm so sorry about what happened to Joseph. The poor young woman who signed him out is devastated. It's not all her fault though. She doesn't know you and the man who came for him had a driver's license in your name. What can I do to help?"

"Well," I said. "I'd like to talk to her, if possible, and I was hoping you might have security footage we could look at."

"You can, and we do, although the police officers already have it. Well, no matter. Please follow me."

She led the way along the corridor to a large office where several more—none of them were wearing habits, but I guess they also were sisters—were seemingly hard at work.

"This is our administrative office," Sister Julia said. "What you need is over here."

We followed her to a desk beside a bank of filing cabinets where yet another sister was working at a computer; her fingers were flying over the keyboard as if her life depended on it.

"A minute, if you please, Sister Frances," Sister Julia said, interrupting the flow.

She looked up, smiled and stood. "Of course."

"This is Sister Mary Frances, Mr. Starke," Sister Julia said. "It was she who signed Joseph out. Sister, this is Mr. Harry Starke and his associate Mr. Ryan. They'd like to talk to you about Joseph."

Then Julia turned to me, offered her hand, and said, "It's been nice to meet you, Mr. Starke, but this place doesn't run itself; I have lots of work to do, so I need to get back to it. If there's anything else I can do to help, please don't hesitate to call me."

I thanked her, shook her hand, and said goodbye, and then turned to Sister Frances.

The smile was gone, replaced by a frown. "Of course," Sister Frances said, her arms folded, "but I must apologize. I should have been more diligent, but the man was so charming, and he had identification. I wouldn't have—"

"It's okay, Sister," I said. "You did what you were supposed to do. You couldn't have known he was an imposter. The thing is though, Joe knows me. He might have gone happily with a stranger, but I think he would have said something."

She looked away and said, "Well, I did think he looked a little apprehensive, but the man put his arm around Joseph's shoulder and said—and I remember exactly—he said, 'Hiya JoJo, you ready to go get some ice cream?' And that's all it took. Joseph was chattering away to him as they headed outside."

"Yes, that would do it," I said. "He loves ice cream."

I thought for a minute, then said, "Can you describe the man who took him? Did you notice anything unusual about him: scars, tattoos, jewelry, anything?"

"No, nothing like that. He was like you in some ways, maybe not quite as tall, but he looked about your age, similar build. He was charming, affable, all smiles, glasses, not much else. Oh, yes, he was wearing tan pants, a black polo shirt, and a ball cap. It was a black one, had a red bill with a big letter A on the front. Atlanta Braves, I think."

"Yes, that sounds right," Bob said. "Would you recognize him if you saw him again, Sister?"

"Yes, I think so."

I nodded. "So, can we see the video footage please?" I had a feeling it wasn't going to be useful, and I was right.

I already knew that security there was not all it should have been, but the folks who ran the place, though not short of funding, liked to spend their cash where they figured it did the most good and didn't consider security a priority. Yes, they had a fair number of CCTV cameras placed at strategic points around the facility, but most of them were in place to keep a watchful eye on their guests, as they like to call them. Still, there were several actual security cameras on the property: one in the lobby—yeah, I know, but it's easier to say lobby than Narthex —and three outside; one at the front of the building set high on a light pole, one on the right side, and another at the rear of the building. *Thank you for that anyway, dear Sisters.*

The cameras at the rear and right side captured nothing. The one in the lobby was in the office, set high—too high—on the opposite wall with its field of view directed through the glass sliding window.

The camera captured the suspect all right, but as I said, it was set too high. The man kept his face lowered so that the camera only picked up the cap and his chin, which was in shadow under the bill of the cap, and several seconds when he signed the release.

"May I suggest, Sister," I said, shaking my head in

frustration, "that you have the camera repositioned some-where off to one side and lower so that it gets a better view of the people at the window."

I had her stop the video several times, but I saw nothing helpful other than the ring on the man's right hand.

"The video is useless for facial recognition, Bob," I said. "But look at the ring."

The sister chimed in. "Oh yes, I forgot. It's a college ring, isn't it?"

"No," Bob said. "It looks like an Army Ranger's ring. They all wear them."

"Yes," I said. "That's what it is, but the stone... shouldn't it be red? This one is black, and that looks like lettering, initials, perhaps."

He stared at it, then nodded and said, "You're right. It's been reworked, but it's fuzzy... I don't think that's lettering, Harry. We need to turn Tim loose on it. Maybe he can enhance the image. I doubt he can do anything with the face. Can we look at the exterior footage please, Sister?"

She tapped the keyboard a couple times and then rolled her seat away so we could see the screen. The images of the suspect coming and going were good qual-ity, clear and sharp, but he knew what he was doing; not once did the camera get a good shot of his face. The vehicle was a late model, black Chevrolet Suburban. Unfortunately, the windows were heavily tinted, and the license plate was muddy, the details obscured; most of them.

"Stop," I said, and she stopped the video.

"Can you enlarge that part?" I said, pointing to the license plate. She could.

"That's a Georgia plate," Bob said. "Fulton County. You can just make out the O and the N, see?"

"Yes, I see," I said. "But there are a dozen counties in Georgia that end in ON. It could be any one of them, or none of them."

"I have a twenty-dollar bill that says it's Fulton. You wanna take the bet?"

I grinned at him. "Atlanta, huh?"

He nodded. "That's what I think."

I nodded. "You may be right, but that"—I pointed at the enlarged image—"is useless. No, keep your money. I'll keep mine."

"So, all we have is the ring, then?" Bob asked, staring at the screen.

I nodded, slowly, also staring at the screen. I had a feeling I was missing something.

"Go back to where they leave the building please, Sister," I said, "and then run it in slow motion."

We, the three of us, watched intently as the scene played out.

He had his arm around Joe's shoulder, his head down as if he was talking to him—which he may well have been —as he escorted Joe to the passenger side of the Suburban, which was facing the convent entrance. Then, at the last moment, the man lifted his head and reached for the door handle, and I spotted something that looked like a smudge on the car window.

"Stop," I said. "Now, enlarge it... There, now stop." *Gotcha, you bastard.*

"There." I pointed to the passenger door window. "See it? It's not clear, but it's the reflection of his face in the window." I looked at Bob. He leaned in closer and squinted.

"You're really reaching, Harry. I see it, but I can't make out any details."

"*You* can't, but when Tim's done with it, you will. I'll need copies please, Sister."

She burned the footage from all five cameras to DVDs. I took them from her, thanked her, and asked her to call me if she remembered anything that might be helpful, and then we left.

"What do you think, Bob? Do you recognize the man on the video footage?" What I was really asking was if it was Nick Christmas or not.

Bob hesitated. We'd worked together long enough I was sure he knew what I meant.

"I don't know," he said. "He looks familiar, but it's not Christmas. He wouldn't get that personally involved."

Bob dropped me off at my father's house in Riverview some thirty minutes later. I left him with the DVDs and instructions to turn them over to Tim the following morning.

Me? I was tired and hungry, but more than anything else I needed to go to the hospital to visit Amanda. How I was going to make that happen, I had no idea; the press was everywhere. Fortunately, Kate arrived a short while after I did. Problem solved.

I spent a few minutes with August and Rose while I ate a pimento cheese sandwich, and then I went in to see my daughter.

She was awake. I picked her up, sat down on the edge of the bed, and held her close.

"Don't squeeze her too hard, Harry," Rose said, smiling, whispering. "She needs to be able to breathe."

"Hey," I said, "I didn't hear you come in."

"I'm sorry," she whispered. "I didn't mean to interrupt. I just wanted to make sure you were all right."

"You're not interrupting, Rose. Come, sit."

She sat down on the edge of the bed beside me, pulled the blanket away from the baby's face with a finger, looked lovingly at her, then sighed and said, "Oh dear, Harry. What are we going to do? First Amanda and now Joe. It's horrible, all of it. You're father's almost out of his mind with worry... about all of you. I've never seen him like this before."

I handed Jade to her, and said, "I know. He doesn't say much. He internalizes everything. I'll talk to him. Not now, tomorrow, maybe even this evening, I promise."

She took the baby from me and held her, cheek to cheek.

"Thank you, Harry. He loves you more than you'll ever know."

"Oh, I know," I said, rising to my feet. "Look, Kate's agreed to take me to the hospital, so I need to go. Can we get together later?"

She nodded. I leaned in and kissed Jade on the forehead. She opened her eyes wide, and I swear she smiled up at me. *Yes, Jade is the right name.*

I looked down at Rose. Her eyes were watering.

"Hey," I whispered. "It will be okay. I promise."

Then I leaned in close and kissed *her* on the forehead. Then I turned and left, my brain churning. I had the certain feeling I'd just made a promise I wouldn't be able to keep.

Kate was waiting when I returned from the bedroom.

"You ready to go?" she asked.

I nodded, then said to August, "I don't know what time I'll be back, but you and Rose need to sleep. Don't wait up for me."

7

MAY 23, 8PM

Erlanger Hospital
"I talked to Chief Johnston," Kate said as we walked to her car. "He's okay with me taking over the missing person case, so I'm in, officially."

"Good," I said, absently. My mind was miles away. I was thinking about Amanda.

"How did it go at the nursing home?" Kate asked as she pushed the starter button.

"Well enough, I suppose. Maybe better than I expected. Kate, this not being able to go to the office is getting to be a real pain in the ass. I need to be able to communicate with my people, especially Tim and Jacque, and..." I was going to say Bob, but then I remembered, and I didn't.

We traveled almost a mile before Kate finally said, "Well, are you going to tell me?"

I wasn't sure if I should tell her or not, but I did.

"I learned something today." I shook my head and said, still not really believing it myself, "Bob's CIA."

For a moment, it didn't register. Then she glanced quickly sideways at me, and said, "*What?* What are you saying? He's a spook? He can't be... You're kidding, right?"

"I wish, but no. He was never a Marine. That was a cover. I'm not even sure he was ever a cop; I didn't get that far. He was twelve years with them, mostly in Afghanistan. Hell, Kate, what happened I still don't know. What I do know, at least according to him, is that he's still on the books; inactive, but still CIA."

I waited for her to say something; she said nothing.

"Comments?" I asked.

"What the hell am I supposed to say? I dated the SOB. He never said a word. What are you—how are you going to handle it?"

"I don't... know. What can I do? He's had my back, and yours, ever since I hired him. Hell, Kate, he's my right hand, my best friend. He owns a forth of my company. The problem is—no, the question is—can I trust him?"

"He's never let you down, Harry—has he?"

"No, never."

"So there's your answer. You can trust him, I think, at least as far as you and your business are concerned."

I sighed, nodded, and said, "It's not like I have a choice, is it?"

She didn't answer. She turned left off East 3rd onto Central and then left again into the Erlanger complex, but instead of taking me to the main entrance, Kate dropped me off on the top floor of the hospital multi-story parking garage. It was a ploy to avoid the press that I was sure would be lying in wait for me, somewhere.

I told her to go home, but she insisted on staying with me. She parked the car, and we took the elevator down to the first floor and from there navigated the corridors to the ICU waiting area where I checked in and was told to go on through. Kate said she'd be in the waiting room.

I stood beside Amanda's bed, took her hand, looked down at her and felt like I was about to throw up. The top of her head down to her earlobes was swathed in bandages. Her eyes, closed, were surrounded by deep, blue-black bruises; her lips cut and swollen; her cheeks and jaw were bruised and covered in cuts, some deep, some little more than scratches.

As far as I could tell, she hadn't moved since I'd left that morning. The tubes had been removed, but she was still receiving medication through an IV.

"Good evening, Mr. Starke."

I turned. "Hello, Dr. Cartwright. How is she?"

Cartwright, a heavy-set man in his mid-forties, pushed his hands deeper into the pockets of his scrubs. "Not much change, I'm afraid. I still have her in an induced coma, and I'll keep her that way for at least another three days, maybe longer, depending upon how the brain swelling responds." He paused, shook his head, and then continued, "She also has three fractured ribs, but they're nothing compared to her head injury. She was lucky, Mr. Starke, very lucky. Another inch to the right and that tree limb would have taken her head off."

"So she's going to be all right, then?"

He looked sideways at me, tilted his head and said, "Will she live, do you mean? Yes."

"What about—"

"Her facial injuries?" he asked, interrupting me.

"That wasn't what—"

"Most of them should heal without scarring," he said again interrupting me. "This one"—he pointed to it—"and this one...I'm not sure, so I've asked Dr. Rohm to look at her."

"I was going to ask about permanent brain damage, Doctor."

"Yes, I know you were." He sighed, shook his head slightly, then said, "Only the good Lord knows that, Mr. Starke. We've done all we can. It's up to her now. Look, I'm sorry, but I have to go. I have other patients. You can stay as long as you like, of course. If you need me, you can contact my nurse. I know you won't, but I do hope you have a good evening." And then he turned and left the room.

I pulled up a chair and sat down, close to the bed, took Amanda's hand in both of mine, put her fingertips to my lips, and closed my eyes. I don't remember much about the next several hours, just a vague recollection of nurses coming and going. I finally woke up to someone gently shaking my shoulder. I was still in my chair but sprawled across the bed, my head on Amanda's chest, though she was unaware of it.

"Mr. Starke," someone whispered.

I came to with a start, looked up into a pair of deep blue eyes. I sat up.

"I'm—"

"It's all right, Mr. Starke," she said. "I just need to take some blood. It won't take but a minute, then I'll leave you alone."

I looked at Amanda. She hadn't moved. I nodded absently, rose to my feet, and stepped away from the bed. I looked at my watch. It was ten after two. *Oh my god, Kate! What the hell was I thinking?*

I waited until the nurse was done poking needles into Amanda's arm, and then I kissed my wife gently on the lips, told her I'd be back soon—I don't know if she heard me or not—and I left. I went to the waiting room: bless her, Kate was still there, asleep in a chair. I shook her gently. She woke with a gasp and stared up at me wide-eyed.

"What time it?"

"It's after two. I'm sorry. I fell asleep too. Look, go on home. I'll call Uber."

"No, Harry. I'll take—"

"*No!*" I said. "You need to go home. I can manage. Now go, please." And she did, though reluctantly.

I had the Uber driver drop me off at my father's house on Riverview. The lights were on and, yes, he was waiting up for me.

"Hey," I said. "You should be in bed."

"I was, but I couldn't sleep. How's Amanda?"

"The same," I said, sitting down on the couch beside him. "No change. I talked to her doctor. He said she'll make it, but he didn't seem too optimistic about her future. God, she's a mess, Dad... No word from the kidnapper yet?"

He was leaning forward, head down, elbows on his knees, cradling a cup of coffee in both hands.

"No."

I put my hand on his shoulder and squeezed it, gently, but said nothing.

"It will soon be light," he said, without looking up. "You should go to bed. Try to get some sleep."

He was right. The events of the past several days had left me drained, and right then, I was really beginning to feel it. My body was aching all over, but all I wanted to do was sit and talk. And that's what we did.

No, I'm not going to bore you with our reminiscing. Let's just say we both managed to depress ourselves to the point where we had to quit and call it a night. It was almost four when I finally fell onto the bed.

Riverview

I awoke with a start; sunlight was streaming in through the window. Bleary-eyed, I rolled over onto my side and grabbed my phone: it was ten after nine. *Oh shit. Damn it all to...*

I rolled onto my back, closed my eyes, and tried to orient myself. It was no good. My mind was refusing to cooperate. *I gotta get a shower.*

I rolled off the bed, realized I was still fully dressed, groaned, sat down on the edge of the bed and slowly began to remove my clothes. I was so stiff, I was barely able to reach my feet. With no little effort, I managed to drag my socks off and stand up. Every muscle in my body protested. I guess the rigors of the past several days had finally caught up with me. I also realized I hadn't worked out in more than a week... *Yeah, and it's not going to happen again any time soon, either.*

I was just about to head for the shower when I heard a gentle knock on the door.

"Hold on. Just give me a minute."

"It's me, Harry," Rose said on the other side of the closed door." I just wanted to make sure you're all right. I have coffee and bagels."

"Oh, okay, that's terrific, thanks, just what I need. I'll get a quick shower and be right there. Fifteen minutes, Rose, that okay?"

"Yes, of course. You'll find toothpaste, toothbrush, and an electric razor in the drawer to the left. When you're done, look in the closet. August went to the pro shop and bought clothes for you."

"Oh, you can't be serious. That's... Good old dad. I was wondering what the heck I was going to wear today. I'll be just a few minutes, Rose."

"Let me have your dirties, and I'll see that they're laundered."

"I love you, Rose."

She laughed, and I hit the bathroom; two minutes later the scalding water hit me. It was so hot it almost took my skin off, and I reveled in it, but not for as long as I would have liked; tempus was fugiting.

I dried off, cleaned my teeth and ran my fingers through my hair; the razor, I didn't bother with. I was already feeling better.

I felt even better when I went to the closet. August had provided everything, and then some: underwear, three pairs of slacks, shirts—all of them white—socks, even a pair of Golfstreet shoes.

August and Rose were waiting for me in the breakfast room. I went straight to the coffee pot, poured myself a huge mug and sat down at the table between them.

"How's Amanda?" Rose asked.

I shook my head and shrugged.

"No change," I said. "Have you heard anything, August?"

He shook his head and stared down into his cup, "No. It's been almost seventy-two hours; I'm beginning to think we won't. That maybe it's not connected to me, us, after all."

"You're the only relative Joe has," I said. "We'll hear from them, even if it's only to demand money, but I'm betting it is connected... Dad, I have a problem. I can't work, not hiding away like this. I need to be able to communicate with my team. I can't do it efficiently by phone and email. If it's okay with you and Rose, I propose to bring them here, well, some of them: Tim and Jacque, Bob, and maybe TJ. For how long, I've no idea: days, maybe weeks. And Tim will need to bring some equipment. You okay with that?"

"Of course," August said, "but I have a computer he can use..." He caught the look on my face.

"Oh, I see," he said.

As bad as the situation was, I had to smile at the thought of Tim trying to work with my dad's circa 2010 PC.

"He'll need some extra room then," August said. "How about the sunroom, will that do?"

I thought about it, then shook my head and said, "I don't think so: too much light. How about the basement, the gym? That's really dark, even during the day."

He nodded.

"Not the gym," Rose said. "Maria is coming today. It's

her day to clean. I'll have her work on the storage room down there. We have two trestle tables, and EPB's network equipment is in there too."

She was talking about the Electric Power Board, one of the largest providers of electrical power in the country. and lately, with internet speeds of 1.0 Gig and up, the fastest fiber optic network supplier too, earning Chattanooga the sobriquet Gig City.

"That will work," I said. "I'll call Jacque and have her put things in motion, but first I need to talk to Tim and let him know what he'll need." *That was a stupid statement. Nobody but Tim knows what he needs, and not even him most of the time.*

"Just give me a couple of minutes," I said. I made the call to Tim and told him to get started putting enough equipment together for an extended stay at Riverview, and that got me wondering how long it would be before press cottoned on to where I was hiding out. *Not very long, I bet.*

Next, I called Jacque and gave her the heads up. Hers was a different situation; she had a full-time staff to keep organized, and there wasn't enough room for all of them at Riverview. Still, it didn't seem to bother her, and she said she'd be with me within the hour. And she was.

Tim arrived an hour after Jacque. His company van loaded to capacity: four fifty-inch monitors, two 5-GPU tower servers, and a whole heap of crap I didn't even know he had, let alone used.

He parked his van outside the basement door, opened its doors, grabbed one of the towers and then, staggering under the weight, he came inside, grinning like a fool.

I just looked at him and shook my head. He never ceased to amaze me.

For those of you who don't, you should know that Tim Clarke runs my IT department. He's the quintessential geek. He's worked for me since before he dropped out of college when he was seventeen. He's tall, skinny, weighs less than 150 pounds, wears glasses, is twenty-seven years old and looks sixteen. I found him in an internet café, just one small step ahead of the law. He was a hacker back then, and still is when he needs to be. I love that boy like a son, but he scares the hell out of me sometimes. You have no idea—I have no idea—exactly what he's capable of, but he is, without a doubt, the most useful and effective member of my staff.

He set the server down on one of the two tables and said, "Hey, Chief. Where's my space?"

"You're in it," I said.

He grinned, shoved his glasses further up the bridge of his nose with a forefinger and said, "Cool. How's Mrs. Starke? She feeling better?"

Tim loved Amanda almost as much as I did, and she, in turn, had a real soft spot for him, and he knew it and played it for all it was worth.

"Not so good, Tim. It's too soon."

"Geez... she's going to be all right though?"

"I hope so. Listen, get yourself organized ASAP and let me know when you're up and running. In the meantime, if you need me, I'll be upstairs in August's office. It's just on the right. Okay?"

"Harry, wait," he said. "Listen, I'm worried about you. Has anyone checked you for radiation?"

I thought about it and decided they hadn't.

"Not that I know of... Oh, you want to do it, right?"

He nodded, frowning.

"Well, you can't, not right now. I—"

He shook his head. "Harry. I need to do it now. That stuff can kill you—"

"Maybe later. Come see me when you're done."

"Mr. Star—"

"I said later, Tim. Now stop bothering me and get your shit together. Were you able to do anything with those images, the ring and the guy that checked Joe out of the nursing home? Bob gave them to you? Where is Bob, by the way?"

"Yes, I was. Yes, he did. He's on his way here now, I think."

"Okay. When can I see them, the photos?"

"You should already have them. I emailed them to you. Didn't you check?"

"No," I said, "I haven't had time. How about CSC and Christmas?"

"I was working on that when you called. I'll get to it again as soon as I get set up."

I nodded and turned to leave.

"Harry, wait. If you won't let me check you out, will you at least take these?"

He took a small plastic bottle from his pocket, opened it, and shook two blue capsules into his hand and offered them to me.

I looked warily at them. "What are they?"

"Prussian Blue. If you have been poisoned, they will help."

"Look, I feel great—not sick, not tired, not... Oh, what the hell."

I took them from him. "Okay. I need water. I'll take them when I get upstairs."

And with that, I left him to it. I was just about to go up the stairs out of the basement when I glanced back; he was already hauling in the second tower. *I guess his desire to check my radiation levels are forgotten, at least for the moment.*

I continued on up the stairs to the powder room and flushed the pills. Yeah, I know, but needs must.

Jacque, bless her, had brought my laptop from the office so I was able to download the images. I did, and I opened them with a certain amount of enthusiasm that quickly turned into disappointment. The image quality was pretty bad. The photo of the ring was fuzzy; the hand was moving when the footage was taken, and the security camera was old, analog, and basic. Tim had tried to enhance it, and he'd succeeded, to a point. I was eighty percent sure it was indeed a US Army Ranger ring. I could just make out the lettering around the outer edge, but the usual red stone emblazoned with 75th had been replaced with a black stone, possibly onyx, with what looked like a central diamond. I'd not seen one like it before.

The image of the reflection in the car window was hardly any better. It too was fuzzy and, yes, I was frustrated. *Maybe Bob... He should be here by now, damn it.*

I picked up my phone and called him.

"I'm outside the front door, Harry."

Rose let him in, and he joined us in the breakfast room.

He greeted August and Rose, looked coolly at me, then nodded.

"Hey," I said. "There's coffee over there. Grab a cup and then come and look at these images."

"No word from the kidnappers?" he asked.

"No."

"So what's the plan, then?"

"See this," I said, pointing to the image of the ring. "What do you make of it?"

He stared at it for a minute, then said, "It looks like a Ranger ring, but unlike any I've ever seen."

"You saw nothing like it in Afghanistan?"

"I just said so, didn't I? If I had, I would have told you."

"What's wrong, Bob?"

"Not a damn thing," he said. "You're going to question everything I say from now on, is that it?"

August and Rose got up and left us alone.

"*No!* Of course not. That was just... just a response... Now wait a minute." I interrupted myself. "I have enough frickin' problems without having to put up with stupid crap from you. I told you yesterday, I'm over it. Now you get over it, and let's concentrate on the job at hand."

He glared at me for a long minute, then nodded, "Okay."

I also nodded and then turned again to the computer screen and the image of the ring.

"So it's a custom job?" I asked.

He shrugged. "It's definitely a Ranger ring, but its significance... I don't know."

I flipped the screen to the image of the reflection.

"What do you think?" I asked. "You said he looked familiar."

He shook his head. "I don't know. It's hard to tell."

"Bob," I stared at the image. "Could this guy be active military?"

He shrugged again. "He could, but I doubt it. The military isn't into kidnapping civilians, especially not—"

"Yeah, I get it," I said interrupting him. "So, if not military, a contractor then, CSC? Christmas is ex-Rangers and a contractor."

"He is, but we know nothing of what he's doing now."

"We will," I said, "as soon as Tim gets his sh—gets his stuff together."

"Yes, well, I have *stuff* I need to do back at the office, so that's where I'll be. Give me a call if anything happens."

I nodded, absently. I was still staring at the image in the car window when he left.

Finally, I gave it up. There was nothing more to be done until Tim was able to work his magic. I was at a dead end, so I went to find August and Rose. I found them in the kitchen, and we sat together and talked, boy how we talked. Talk about life flashing before your eyes.

Around eleven, I followed Rose into their bedroom where Jade was hanging out, watched while she changed her, intending to grab a few quality moments with her myself when she was finished.

It was while I was with Rose and Jade, at eleven-forty-four, that August got the call. No, I didn't hear it, not first-hand anyway.

August walked into the bedroom just as I was about to take Jade from Rose.

"They just called," he said. "They said that if I don't drop the case, they'll kill Joe. That was it. That was all they said."

I looked at him. His face was white. I put my hand on his arm. "Take it easy," I said. "Now we know. Now we have something to go on. Was it a man?"

"I couldn't tell. The voice was electronically altered."

I closed my eyes for a moment, thinking. "Damn!" I said, more to myself than to August. "I hope Tim got it."

Fortunately, Tim was ahead of the game and was already monitoring all incoming calls.

What the caller actually said was, "If you want to see your brother again, stay the hell away from Lewis Walker."

Tim had a voiceprint and said it was indeed a man's voice: he would know, I guess. Me? If it was, I couldn't tell. August was right: the voice sounded like something out of one of those old movies. The call—with no caller ID—lasted exactly six seconds; too short for Tim to trace.

"Any idea where it might have originated?" I asked.

Tim shook his head. "Sorry." *Yeah, me too.*

"Why Walker, August?" I asked. "It makes no sense."

"Actually, it does. Walker is the whole case. Without him, it's all circumstantial. Cronin, Christmas' attorney, maintains that CSC is clean, that Walker was working alone. Without Walker, if we can't find him, or if he's dead, I can't make the case against CSC."

Tim nodded, and said, "I get that, but now we know different. Somebody abducted Joe, and now we know why; to put pressure on you. We also know, because of the connection to Walker, that Christmas is behind it. Isn't that enough?"

"No, Tim," August said. "Unless you can tie that call, or even the voice, to a person, it's all circumstantial; it means nothing... Well, it means something, but only to us."

"I think Walker's dead," I said. "It's what I would do if I was Christmas. If Walker is that important, I'd have put him away the minute the system turned him loose. Yeah, he's dead, for sure."

"I don't think so," August said. "But let's say you're right, in which case, why take Joe?"

He had me there.

"There's only one way to find out. I need to talk to Christmas, and quickly. Every hour we lose is critical, but first I need to talk to Tim, and I need to get Bob back here."

MAY 24, AFTERNOON

Riverview
    I went to the basement and found Tim sitting in front of four huge monitors—two over two—banging away at one of three keyboards. He was wearing earbuds and oblivious to everything other than the stream of data scrolling down one of the screens.

I stood behind him and tapped him gently on the shoulder. If he felt it, he didn't show it. I tapped again, a little harder.

"*Wait,* please." Not for a second did he take his eyes off the screen. So, I waited... and I waited.

Finally, I pulled one of the earbuds out. He swung around, reaching over his shoulder, trying to locate the missing bud.

"*Harry!* I knew you were there, but I couldn't stop what I was trying to—" He shook his head, frustrated. "You wouldn't understand."

"Try me," I said.

"I was, as they say on Star Trek, running a Level One

diagnostic. I was making sure everything is running as it should."

Star Trek. I stared down at him. *Are you kidding?*

"Well?" I asked.

He nodded, did his thing with his glasses, and grinned up at me.

"I'm ready, Captain, to explore strange new worlds..." He caught the look I was giving him. "Er, sorry. What do you need Cap—I mean, Harry."

I rolled my eyes. "I need information: Nicholas Christmas and his company, CSC. When can I have it?"

"Well, let me think." He grabbed the glasses from his face and a microfiber cloth from the table, polished them vigorously, threw down the cloth, rammed the glasses back in place and poked them with a forefinger. "A couple of hours?" he asked, tentatively.

"You have one hour. I'll be back with Bob and Kate at two-thirty, and you'd better have something for me."

He frowned, squinted. I thought for a minute he was going to burst into tears, but he didn't. Instead, he grinned up at me and said, "Aye, Captain."

I shook my head and left him banging away at the keys and twittering to himself, "He wants the impossible, Geordi."

I didn't know who Geordi was, but I suspected he had something to do with the Enterprise. *Oh well, 'that's gotta be worth a couple of pages in someone's book.'* I smiled at the thought. *Tim would be proud of me.* I continued up the stairs to August's office where I made the call to Bob and asked him to join me.

I also called Kate because, one: I needed to know if

there had been any developments with the missing person case. There hadn't. Two: I asked her to also join me at Riverview because she needed to know what was going on and... well, I hate having to repeat myself.

Next, I went to see Jacque.

Jacque had taken over August's office but not his vintage computer. That, she'd moved temporarily to a credenza off to one side of the room. She was seated in August's great leather desk chair—the damn thing is even bigger than mine—her phone to her ear. She looked up at me, smiled, held up a finger and mouthed, "give me one minute."

I nodded and turned to leave. She tapped sharply on the desk and pointed to the chair in front of it.

I smiled at her and sat down. She continued her call for what could only have been twenty or thirty seconds, then set her phone on the desk and looked across it at me.

"So," she said. "I see from the look that you want to talk. You've been like a bear with a sore tooth since I got here. What's up?"

"Oh, not a thing," I said, sarcastically.

"There you go," she said, leaning forward and putting her forearms on the desk, her hands clasped together. "Like a bear..." She paused, tilted her head to one side, then nodded and smiled at me.

"Look, Harry," she said. "What you did was unbeliev-able. You saved us all. How you did it—how you held it together—I don't know. And then Amanda getting hurt. If it was Wendy, I'd be out of my mind. And now there's Joseph kidnapped. What else is there? What else *could* there be?"

"Thanks, Jacque. Yeah, I do have a lot on my mind." *And now I have to tell you about Bob.*

"So you wan' to unload? Talk to me."

There it was, the Jamaican accent.

"It's Bob."

She sat up straight. "What about him?"

I hesitated. Was I doing the right thing? Did it really matter? *Ah, the hell with it. If I don't tell her, I'm as bad as Bob, keeping it a secret all this time.*

"He's CIA, Jacque. Always has been."

Her eyes widened, Her mouth opened and then shut again.

"Apparently, they let him off active duty back in 2006, but they never removed him from the books. He's inactive, but still CIA."

"How'd you find dis out?" she asked, very quietly.

"He told me, yesterday. He didn't seem to think it was a big deal. But it is: not the fact that he's CIA though. It's that he didn't tell us. He didn't tell *me.*"

"And you did a background check on him, right?"

"Yes, of course."

"And?"

"Nothing... well, nothing about the CIA. I asked him why not, and he said it was a need-to-know thing, covered by the Espionage Act."

"Tell me this, Harry: Would you have hired him if you'd known?"

I thought for a minute, then nodded. "Yes, I would have."

She leaned back in her chair, smiling, her arms high, hands palm up, like Buddha. "So it's okay then; no foul.

He's still Bob Ryan. Yes, he's got a murky past, but he worked for the government, not the Mafia, so what's your beef?"

"Well, he—" I stopped, stared at her, and then I realized she was right, and I nodded.

"You're right, Jacque. You always are. Thank you."

And that was the end of it, at least as far as I was concerned.

I looked at my watch, it was one-fifteen.

"They'll be here soon, Kate and Bob," I said. "I'll need you to join us downstairs."

She nodded. "No problem."

"There are some folding chairs in the sunroom, let's grab a couple and head on down." And we did.

They arrived together at a little after two; Kate had called Bob and arranged to pick him up, and they didn't look happy. In fact, I got the distinct impression that they'd been arguing. That being so, I decided to put it to bed once and for all.

"Okay, you two," I said, "outside. We need to talk."

I led the way out onto the patio and pointed to a round, teak table and chairs. "Take a seat."

We sat, and I continued, "Okay, we don't have time to fool around like this, so I'll make it short. We, the three of us, have a problem, and we have to solve it... now."

I looked at each of them in turn. Bob sat back in his chair, his arms folded, his expression blank. Kate stared stoically back at me but said nothing.

"Bob," I continued, "I've done a lot of thinking these last twenty-four hours, and I think I understand why you weren't forthcoming about your past. I don't like it, but what's done is done. You haven't changed; you are who you are, what you are, and I love you like a brother, so I'm over it. Kate, we all have to work together, so you need to get over it too."

She glanced sideways at him. Her face softened. She looked back at me with just the hint of a smile and nodded.

"Bob?" I asked.

He shrugged. "As far as I'm concerned, there never was a problem. Now, is that it? Can we go back to work?"

Just like that? I wonder...

"We can," I said. "Let's go talk to Tim."

JACQUE HAD ARRANGED the seating in a half-circle with Tim's computers at the center and was already seated next to him. He'd spun his chair around and was sitting with his back to his monitors, flipping through screens on his iPad. He was, as usual, lost in a world of his own.

"Hey, Tim," I laid a hand on his shoulder, to get his attention. "You in there?"

He turned, looked up, grinned at me and nodded.

"Good," I said. "What do you have? I need to know everything there is to know about Christmas, CSC and their operations."

He stared down at the iPad, scratched his ear, then said, thoughtfully, "The last couple years are pretty murky... Okay, this is what I have so far. Nicholas James Christmas was born in Clarksville, Tennessee, on October 7, 1974, the son of Theresa and Jordan Wesley Christmas, a U.S. Army major. He grew up in Clarksville and graduated from the Clarksville Academy, a private prep school, in 1992. He attended the University of Georgia on an ROTC scholarship and graduated in 1996 in the top five percent of his class. Then he was commissioned into the United States Army as a 2nd Lieutenant in 1997 and was immediately recruited into Military Intelligence.

"He applied to become a Ranger a year later and was accepted into Ranger School at Fort Benning, GA, in January 1999 where he specialized in counterintelligence. On graduating from Ranger School, he was promoted to 1st Lieutenant and deployed to Beirut.

"In October 2001, right after 911, he was promoted to captain and was with the Iraq invasion force in March 2003. He was in Iraq for nine months and then in November 2004, he was deployed to Afghanistan where he did three tours, almost back-to-back, three years in all. He resigned his commission within three months after returning home from his third tour in March 2008. He founded CSC a year later in March 2009."

Tim took a drink of water from his Star Trek water bottle. Then he continued reading from his iPad.

"Okay, so onto CSC, and this is where it gets murky. It was a tough one. What little information I could find about Christmas Security Concepts—CSC—is buried deep." He paused, looked up at me, scratched the top of his head with one finger, then continued.

"CSC Incorporated, from what I was able to find, is a small, covert private military company that provides security services to the United States federal government on a contractual basis. The corporate offices are in

Atlanta... well, Marietta, actually. But they have a satellite location. It appears to be a training facility of some sort—in the Copperhill, Tennessee area with access to Martin Campbell Field—where they keep a Huey helicopter and a Beech 90 King Air jump plane."

"Copperhill?" I asked. "There's nothing there but a few hundred people. Why there?"

"Just that," Bob said. "It's remote, desolate country. Ideal for training purposes and... other activities."

"Other activities?" I said. "You're talking drugs, trafficking, smuggling?"

He shrugged. "To say the least. You can't do any of that crap in Atlanta."

I nodded. "Maybe that's where they're keeping Walker or Joe."

"Could be," Bob said. "Can you pull it up, Tim?"

He could, so he spun his seat to face the monitors, and in just a few seconds, we were looking at a satellite view of the area.

"That's Campbell Field, there," Tim said, pointing.

"What's all that mess there, to the left?" Kate said.

"All of that area was once dedicated to copper mining," Tim said. "What you're seeing—the lakes—is called Gypsum Pond, all part of the devastation the mining caused. I'm thinking that, right there, is the CSC compound." Tim pointed to what looked like a collection of prefabricated buildings just to the south of three fairly large lakes and west of the south end of the airfield.

He leaned back in his chair, adjusted the position of his glasses, then said, "See? There's a dirt road leading from the complex to the airfield."

"Hmm, interesting," I said. "Can you enlarge it? I'd like to see what they have there."

He did, and I could see there were six buildings in all, each having a steel roof.

"I wonder, how big an area do they own?" I said. "Surely it's not just the compound."

The compound, and that's surely what it was, was surrounded by what looked like a steel security fence with light poles set at regular intervals. At night, the place would be ablaze with light. *I bet there are cameras on those poles.*

"If they're training mercenaries," Bob said, "I'd say they use the entire area around and including the lakes, from the road east of the airport to... hell, who knows? It has to be at least five or six square miles, most of it forested."

"What else could they be doing?" I said. "That's quite a facility. That one building looks to be big enough to house a small army." I sighed and shook my head. "Go on, Tim. What else did you find?"

"Yes, sir! Okay. So, since 2009 when the company was founded, the group has provided services to the CIA."

I couldn't help but glance sideways at Bob. If he saw the look, he ignored it.

"I could find very little information about the company staffing," Tim continued. "The numbers— payroll, social security, and so on—are unavailable, classified. I stopped short of hacking into... Well, if that's what you want..." He paused, expectantly.

I said nothing.

"Okay then," he said. "So, as far as I can tell, I'd say there are less than fifty official employees and maybe as many more off the books. Soldiers of fortune, I guess you'd call them. Most of them seem to be deployed: here in the U.S. and in Afghanistan and Iraq."

He paused and grinned at me. "You wanna know how I know that?" He pushed his glasses further up the bridge of his nose.

I glanced over at Kate. She nodded.

"Tell us, Tim," I said.

"I followed the money, well, some of it—which wasn't easy, I can tell you—some of it I couldn't... Well I can, but it's all buried in off-shore accounts, shell companies, you know. It will take a little time. So, anyway, I was, however, able to get a handle on his immediate senior staff. They're all former Army Rangers.

"They are: ex-Sergeant Henry 'Hank' Johnson, ex-Sergeant Jessica Roark, John 'Johnny' Pascal, James 'Bunny' Hare, Herman 'Herm' Garcia, and"—he paused, for effect—"ex-Corporal Lewis Walker."

Bob spoke up. "I'd say that's his entire team from Afghanistan. I met Johnson maybe a half dozen times, and Roark three times, no four. She's one tough b—cookie."

"Ex-Sergeant Johnson is an enigma," Tim said. His title is now Executive Vice President and, from all accounts he's Christmas' second in command, but take a look at this photo of him." He put it up on one of the screens. "The man's a hulk, a brute. He was discharged from the army a year later after Christmas in November

2010 and joined his former CO at CSC where he is now VP of Field Operations."

"Yeah," Bob said, "That's Hank all right. I always figured the two were strange bedfellows. Christmas was an intelligent, well-educated military officer, and he talked to him as if he was his equal. Johnson, on the other hand, was less well-educated but was a street smart, dedicated soldier of fortune. I'd say he's Nick's fixer."

Tim nodded, and continued, "In February 2009, after conducting more than fifty interviews, Christmas hired Julia Stein, a somewhat gifted accountant. She was then thirty-two and held two master's degrees in finance and banking. As far as I can tell, she's clean: no criminal record, no debts, nor even a parking ticket."

Tim nodded, looked up at me, and said, "That's all I have right now. If you want, I can dig into Johnson and the rest of the team, but it will—"

"No, Tim," I said, interrupting him. "Not now anyway. What I need you to do is upgrade the security system here and at the office, and I need it done right away. Get hold of—oh hell, you know that better than I do. Just do it, okay?"

"I'll get right on it," Tim said. "Budget?"

"Since when did you care about such things? Just do it."

He grinned at me. I shook my head, then glanced at my watch; it was almost two-thirty.

"Okay," I said. "Bob, you and I will go visit Christmas, now, this afternoon. It's what, a hundred miles to Marietta? It's a straight shot on I-75. We can be there in ninety minutes, say by five anyway. The rest of you, get some rest. Who knows what tomorrow will bring?"

"What if he's not there?" Jacque asked.

I looked at Bob, quizzically.

He nodded. "You have his number, Tim?" he asked.

Tim gave it to him, and he punched it into his phone, then put it on speaker. It rang a couple of times before being answered. The voice was female.

"CSC. How can I help you?"

"Tell Nick that his old buddy Bob Ryan is on the phone."

The other end of the line was silent and stayed that way for at least a couple of minutes, then, "Well, well, now ain't that a blast from the past? How are you, Bob?"

"Oh, you know how it is, Nick. Listen, I need to see you this afternoon. I have a proposition for you. I'll be there by five-thirty. You gonna be there?"

"Yeah, but what's the rush? Wouldn't tomorrow be—"

"For you, maybe, but not for me. It has to be today."

"So what is it you want, Bob?"

"Not over the phone, Nick. You know how it is, probably better than most."

There was a long pause. We could hear him breathing, then, "Okay. Five-thirty. I'll be waiting." He disconnected, and the room was quiet.

"You ready, then?" Bob asked.

"Yes," I said. "Almost but give me just a minute."

I went upstairs to my room, swilled water over my face, dried off, then I slipped into my shoulder holster, then put on a dark green, lightweight golf jacket. I checked my VP9 then slipped it into the holster under my arm. My backup, a tiny Sig P938 in a sticky holster, I slid into my waistband at the small of my back. I love that little gun, a tiny replica of the classic, .45 Colt 1911. In fact, I have two of them. The one I carry as a backup and a second that, on rare occasions, I carry in an ankle holster, but not that day.

Now I was ready to go.

Marietta, GA

We were late, not by much, but enough to make me more than a little antsy. We turned off the Interstate, right onto Marietta Parkway and then right again onto Kennestone Circle where we found CSC housed in a large warehouse with offices facing the street.

We parked in front of the main entrance, sat for a moment discussing strategy—of which we really didn't have any—and then went inside where we found a sliding glass window. Beyond the window, seated at a desk, was an incongruously big man with a shaved head.

"Hello, Hank," Bob said, through a talk-through hole. "Long time no see."

The man looked up from what he was doing and smiled... Ha, it was more snarl than smile, eyes half closed, and tight lips over two rows of teeth a barracuda would have been proud of.

"Bob Ryan, no less," the giant said, rising to his feet.

"Nick said you were coming. Hold tight, I'll let you through."

He pushed a button under the sliding window. There were two loud clunks as the bolts from inside of the steel door slid back and hit their stops.

"Come on through. He's waiting for you."

He was indeed waiting for us, and he didn't look pleased about it.

He was standing just inside his open office door.

"Bob, my old friend," he said, holding out his hand. He sounded affable, but there was an edge to his voice. "How the hell are you?" he asked, not waiting for an answer. "Come on in. What have you been up to? It's been what, ten years?"

Christmas was a tall, slim man, maybe six-one, with dark brown hair and a neatly trimmed beard and mustache. He was wearing a dark blue business suit that must cost every penny of five grand with a white shirt and a red and black striped tie. His office was plush: a huge walnut desk, bookcase behind it, two leather Chesterfield chairs in front, and some obviously expensive artwork on the walls. The suit and the office seemed more the accouterments of a banker than that a soldier of fortune.

"Nick," Bob said, with a quick, single nod as he gripped his hand. There was nothing friendly about it. "Yes, ten years, give or take. You're looking well."

"Thank you," Christmas said, as he looked at me. "Who's your friend?"

Why do I get the distinct impression that you already know? I thought.

"Harry Starke, Nick Christmas," Bob said, never taking his eyes off Christmas.

Christmas narrowed his eyes, tilted his head a little to one side, then nodded slowly and said, "Holy cow. *The* Harry Starke? The Harry Starke that only two days ago saved Chattanooga from nuclear destruction? Lord! I *am* honored."

The son of a bitch is mocking me.

He offered me his hand. I almost ignored it, but then I thought better of it and took it. His fingers closed on mine like a steel vise. If I'd been expecting it... well, I wasn't, and I stared into a pair of taunting, icy blue eyes as he increased the pressure. It hurt like hell, but I gave no sign of it.

"That's enough, Nick," Bob said. "You've nothing to prove."

The pressure slackened, enough for me to be able to return the compliment, and I did. He didn't give an inch, but the smile turned humorless, and I knew I'd taken him by surprise. Oh yeah, I know, it was childish, but I enjoyed the hell out of the look in his eye. I turned him loose.

"Not bad, Harry," he said, flexing his fingers. "Not bad at all. You're obviously a man to be reckoned with." This time the tone was one of contempt.

"Okay," he said, brightly. "Please sit down. What can I do for you? Oh, forgive me: would you like something to drink? Scotch, perhaps?" he asked looking at me and smirking.

Bob and I shook out heads and sat down, side by side in the two Chesterfields. They were so low, I could barely see over the edge of his desk. So, no sooner had my rear end settled into the leather than I stood up again.

"What?" Christmas asked, grinning.

"You know what," I said, grabbing a straight-backed dining chair from the rear of the room and setting it down to the right of the Chesterfield I'd just vacated. I sat down, nodded, and said, "Now, can we get on with it?"

Before we could, however, Bob also decided his chair was too low, and he stood up and looked around. Unfortunately, there were no more chairs.

Christmas leaned forward, picked up his desk phone, tapped the screen and said, "Dana. Would you please bring my guest a chair? Thank you." He leaned back, and again made with the smile.

Dana brought the chair, and Bob sat down. "Okay, Nick," he said. "You've had your fun. Now stop playing stupid games. We've come a long way."

"Ah, Bob. You haven't changed at all. Still the brusque, no-nonsense company man. Are you still with them, by the way?"

"No, I'm Harry's partner, but you knew that, right?"

Nick nodded.

Bob looked around the office, and said, "You've done well for yourself, Nick. The security business must be treating you well."

"I can't complain," he said, his smile broadening. "Business is good. What's to complain about?"

"Yeah," Bob said. "You always were one lucky son of a bitch. Now you have your own private army, so I heard."

"What do you want, Ryan? You said it wouldn't wait until tomorrow. So tell me."

He leaned forward, placed his elbows on the desk, clasped his hands together, and did his best to be sincere. I wasn't convinced, but it was then that I noticed the ring on the middle finger of his left hand.

"Nice ring," I said. "Army Rangers, I think, but a little unusual. Custom?"

His eyes narrowed as he frowned. He looked down at the back of his hand, balled his fingers into a fist, the ring on top. The large diamond sparkled darkly. He placed the fist into the palm of his other hand and screwed it back and forth as if polishing the ring; he wasn't. The gesture was pure threat.

"Yes, custom. A gift."

"Do all of your men have them?"

"Several do. Why do you ask?"

"Oh," I said, feigning surprise. "No reason. It was just a thought."

And then something totally unexpected happened; something inside me snapped. I don't know if it was because of what was going on with Amanda and Joe, but whatever it was, I suddenly realized I was done pussy-footing around.

I leaned forward, looked him right in the eyes, and said, "No! The hell it was just a thought. Five days ago, one of your thugs kidnapped my uncle Joseph. I know he was one of yours because he was wearing an identical ring. Then you called my father and told him to drop the case against your company or you'd kill Joe. I want to know where the hell he is, and I want to know right now, you self-satisfied, preening, arrogant son of a bitch."

I reached inside my jacket, pulled my VP9 from its holster, stood, walked around the desk and slammed the muzzle of the gun down hard on his knee.

"Now, you piece o' shit," I said snarling. "Where is he? Tell me or I'll put you on sticks for the rest of your life."

That's all it took, right? Wrong. He simply leaned back in his chair and smiled up at me.

"Harry," he said, quietly. "I have no idea what you're talking about. I made no such call, and I don't have your uncle. Now, put that thing away before you hurt someone."

I saw red. I took a half-step sideways and slammed the barrel of the heavy gun against the side of his head. He fell sideways out of the chair and lay wide-eyed on his back, both hands to his head, blood streaming through his fingers.

"For God's sake, Harry," Bob yelled as he jumped to his feet. "What the hell do you think you're doing?"

He came around the desk like Tony Gonzales; he was flying. He hit me with his shoulder, and the next thing I knew, I slammed backward into the bookcase. I went down like a sack of garbage. And then I was up again, boiling mad and swinging.

"You son of a bitch, Ryan."

"*Hey!*" Bob yelled as the VP9 missed his ear by less than an inch. "Hey—hey! Calm down, Harry. For God's sake stop."

I stopped, one hand on the desk, breathing heavily, the other gripping the VP9 at my side.

"Step, back, Harry," Bob said, quietly.

"You dumb shit," I said, as I staggered around the desk toward him. "I almost frickin' shot you."

"No, you didn't. If that's what you intended, you would have. Now calm down, damn it. Look what you've done."

I looked. Christmas was lying on his back, groaning, blood seeping through his fingers onto the carpet.

Dana rushed into the room. "What's going on? Oh my God. You've killed him." She grabbed the desk phone.

Bob took it gently from her.

"It's okay," he said to her. "Nick is okay. He's just hurt a little, is all."

"Get out, Dana, I'm fine," Christmas said, using the edge of the desk to pull himself to his feet.

"Do you want me to call an ambulance?" she asked.

"Hell no. I told you, I'm fine. Now go and leave me alone. These two *gentlemen* are leaving."

She left, closing the door behind her.

Christmas sat down at his desk. He pulled open a drawer and removed a fistful of paper napkins from a box and held them to his ear, which was still bleeding. Then he reached under his desk and did something we couldn't see, but I could guess what it was; he'd called for help.

"You," he said, looking at me. "Do you have any idea what you've just done, or who and what you did it to? I don't know where your frickin' uncle is; I don't have him. But I do know where to find you, Starke. You're screwed;

you too, Ryan. Now get the hell out of my office, both of you, before my men arrive and throw you out."

I took a deep breath, then said, "You're lying, Christmas. I know you are. Now, I'll make you the same deal you offered my father: turn Joe loose or I'll kill you."

I heard the door open behind me. I never took my eyes of Christmas, who held up his hand, and said, "Take it easy, Hank These two are just leaving, show them out."

"Hell, Boss," the giant said. "You're bleedin', man. These sons-a-bitches—"

"It's okay," Christmas said, interrupting him. "I'm okay. Just show them out and see that they leave the premises."

"Hey, dickhead," the giant said to me. "You going to put that thing away, or do you want me to take it away from you?"

I turned to face him. I was boiling; not good. "Do it," I said, pointing the VP9 at his right knee, my finger on the trigger.

"Whoa," Bob said, stepping between us. "That's enough, both of you. Harry, we've got to get the hell out of here. Johnson, you stand still, right where you are, or I'll bust that shiny head. Nick, this ain't over. You can't pull your kind o' shit in this country. You turn the man loose, or by God..." And he grabbed my arm and hauled me out of the office.

"What the hell was that about, Harry?" he asked, as he closed the car door. "Those people are killers. You can't treat them that way."

I punched the starter button, with way more force than I needed, slammed the gear shift into drive, and squealed the tires out of the complex out onto Kenne-stone Circle, heading for the Interstate.

By the time we hit the on-ramp, I'd calmed down, just a little.

"Bob, I can't keep doing this shit... I need to go and see Amanda. Before I do, though, I'll drop you off at Riverview. We're going to have to resolve this thing, and quickly. I'll have Rose make up a bed on the couch. You can have my room."

"Oh, don't talk shit, Harry. I'll take the couch."

11

FRIDAY, MAY 25, EARLY

R **iverview**
Bob did indeed sleep on the couch that night, but he didn't get to it until well after midnight. He was on the couch watching TV when I returned from the hospital.

Amanda? No change. I don't think she'd even moved since the last time I'd seen her. I didn't stay long; there wasn't any point. I talked to one of the nurses, but she could tell me nothing... or maybe she just wouldn't. I didn't know. So finally, I stood, leaned over the bed and gently kissed her lips, then looked at her face. It was beautiful—badly damaged, and expressionless, but beautiful just the same. The only encouraging sign was that she was breathing steadily, on her own.

I have to say, I was more than a little pleased to find Bob still awake: I needed someone to talk to, and talk we did. We sat together, reminiscing about the past... No, not the events of the past week. I wasn't ready for that, not yet. And we did a little drinking... No, not a lot, just a couple, more for something to do with our hands than... well, you get the idea.

Talking together about nothing and everything was something Bob and I had never done before. Why, I don't know. It was just something we never did. That night, however, I learned a lot about Bob and, if I'm truthful, myself too. It didn't take long for me to figure out that Bob never really was who I thought he was; it was as if I was getting to know a whole new person.

I always knew he was smart... Well, smartass might be a better way to describe him, but he was more than that, way more. I don't know whether or not he was glad to drop the pretense, but I soon realized I was talking to a highly intelligent, highly trained CIA officer, not the rough and tumble, hard-charging ex-cop I'd always thought him to be.

It was inevitable then, that the conversation turned to the present situation: first Nick Christmas and then my missing uncle.

"You do know that they have Joe, don't you, Bob?" I asked.

"It's possible," he said.

I shook my head. "No. Christmas has him. I'm sure of it. I'm also just about convinced that he's at the facility up there in the mountains, and if he is, I'm going to get him."

"If he's there, sure. If he's not; what then?"

"I don't know," I said, "and right now my brain feels like concrete..." I thought for a minute, then said, "There's nothing we can do until morning, so I'm going to turn in. You sure you want to sleep on the couch?"

"I'll be fine. Go to bed, Harry. Get some sleep. We'll talk in the morning."

I nodded and left him, staring out of the window.

I woke early the following morning... No, that's not quite true: I rose early the following morning—at just after five-thirty—having slept very little. I decided to forgo my morning run and made coffee and bagels instead. I filled a couple of mugs, stuck half a toasted, buttered bagel between my teeth, and went into the lounge where Bob was still asleep.

"Hey," I said. "Wake up. I've brought coffee."

He didn't move, not even the flicker of an eyelid. I set the mugs down on the coffee table and gave him a poke with my finger.

"Hey, wake up."

"Geez, Harry," he said, blearily. "Don't you ever sleep? You put sugar in that?"

"You don't take sugar."

He blinked up at me, swung his feet off the couch and sat up.

"Don't ever ask me to do that again," he said. "I had maybe five minutes; the couch is too damn short. Yeah, yeah, I know. It never was meant for sleeping, right?"

"You're full of it, you know that?" I asked. "I came in here twice during the night to check on you; you were out cold both times."

He cut me a weird look over the rim of his mug, and

said, "Well, the coffee's good anyway. How long have you been up?"

"Most of the night, thinking."

"So, you been thinking, huh? What did you come up with? Do we have a plan?"

It was a question I'd asked myself many times during the night, and the truth was, I didn't. One thing I knew for sure, though.

"We need to go in there and get Joe out," I said.

"We don't even know if he's there. Hell, we don't even know for sure that Christmas has him."

"True," I said, "but I think he does have him, and that facility up at Copperhill is where I'd hide him, if it were me. Look, we won't know, not until we go and look." I paused for a second.

He sipped on his coffee and looked at me expectantly.

I checked my watch. "It's almost seven. There's no point in doing this now. We need to wait for the others. Go get yourself cleaned up, and then we'll have breakfast. You can use my shower. When you're done, you'll find underwear and golf shirts in the closet. You'll find them a little tight, but they should work for you; I wear my shirts loose. They're all new. August bought them for me from the club."

He looked at me skeptically. "You can't be serious. I'm twice the man you are."

"Don't you wish," I said. "Go on, get out of here. You're stinking up the place."

12

FRIDAY, MAY 25, MORNING

Riverview

Kate was the first to arrive, then Jacque and Tim arrived together. Jacque had given him a ride home; having left his van at the back of the house. By the time they, Jacque and Tim, had arrived it was almost nine, and I was pacing the kitchen floor.

"You need to calm down," Bob said.

Calm down? Me? The man's on his third cup of coffee.

"Don't you look at me like dat," Jacque said, dumping her heavy bag and laptop on the kitchen table. "I can't just up and leave the office any time I want, you know."

I sighed, nodded, and told everyone to grab coffee, bagels, whatever, and get downstairs. I'd be with them just as soon as I'd said good morning to Jade.

Yes, I know what you're thinking: why hadn't I done that earlier? Because Rose, God love her, had warned me in no uncertain terms that I couldn't. She wanted the baby to sleep uninterrupted.

So, at nine-fifteen, she finally allowed me to enter the

bedroom and hold my daughter. That was something I'd not yet gotten used to, and I couldn't help but wonder if I ever would.

After a while, Rose came in to check on us.

"You look like you're holding a basket of eggs," she said. "Here, let me."

She took the baby from me, and I received my first practical instruction on parenting. Did I learn a lot? Hell no, and I have to admit I was glad to hand Jade over to her grandmother, kiss her on the nose—the baby, not Rose—and make my way back to the kitchen.

Amanda, what are you doing to me? Please get well?

I grabbed my fourth cup of coffee and headed downstairs to join the others. Tim was already banging away at the keyboard. The top two monitors were both showing the area of wilderness surrounding Gypsum Pond Campbell Field. One was a wide satellite view of the entire six square miles, it's dirt tracks, forested areas, the three lakes, the airfield, and the compound. The second monitor was showing a closeup of the compound. The detail was amazing.

"I know that's not Google Maps," I said. "You've tapped into a direct feed, right?"

"Oh yeah," Tim said, enthusiastically. "Well, not quite. What you're seeing is a recording I made fifteen minutes, or so, ago. The satellite designated EIO209C passes just to the west every ninety minutes. It's in optimum position for less than ten minutes, so what you're seeing is already old news. We'll get another update in... sixty-eight minutes."

I stepped closer, studied the compound, looking for

details, for anything that might give me a hint as to what was going on there. But there was little to see, other than several vehicles parked close to the biggest of the six buildings, including a black SUV, a pickup truck, a Jeep Wrangler, and a box van.

"What do you think, Bob?" I asked. "Can it be done?'

"It can, but it won't be easy. They won't know we're coming, so we'll have the element of surprise, but see those boxes on the light poles? Those are cameras. If I know Nick, they cover every inch of the compound. That area outside the fence; it's a hundred feet of open ground all around the fence. There's no way to cross it without being seen." He paused, thought for a minute, then said, "Brute force might be the answer, but it would be dangerous."

"Brute force?" I asked. "What are you thinking?"

"See this track here?" He stepped up, pointed to a spot on the monitor screen. "We can access it here." Again, he pointed. "From there it's a straight run to the gate. We'd need a heavy vehicle to smash through the gate, but it could be done."

I stared at the screen, picturing what Bob was suggesting in my mind.

"Can you zoom in tighter, Tim?" I asked.

He tapped the keyboard. The gate grew larger, and I shook my head.

"It would take a tank to get through that; the fence too. No, we'll have to think of something else."

I stared some more. It didn't get any better. I sighed, shook my head again, and said, "ease out a little please,

Tim. Whoa. Stop. Right there. What's that? Go back in a little."

I was looking at what I thought might be a drainage ditch at the rear of the row of buildings. It wasn't. It was just a shallow depression.

"It's time for the satellite to make another pass. I can give you some real-time footage."

"Oh shit. Look, there... and there. Zoom in, Tim. Shit, those are armed men. They must be guards. They're heading for the fence. They... yes, they're patrolling the perimeter. How come we haven't seen that before?"

"I'd say because they're on a schedule," Bob said.

"Harry," Tim said, looking sheepish. "Before we go any farther, there's something you should know. I did a little research when I got home last night. Everything you're looking at, the entire area, is government property. Department of Defense, to be precise."

"Oh hell," Bob said. "That complicates matters. How the hell did Nick get access to that, I wonder?"

"It makes no difference," I said. "We have to do this no matter who owns the damned property."

"True," Bob said, "but it means the security up there will be even more sophisticated than we first thought."

I shrugged. "Probably. It looks tough, I agree."

I really didn't see that it made much difference. We were planning a raid on a secure property, sure, but the said property was being used for criminal activities. I hoped, and at that point, the only way I could prove that was to find Joe and get him out. If he wasn't there, then yes, my team and I, if we were caught, would be in deep trouble. But thinking back to those days, I really didn't have a choice. As I said before, we had to do it. Well, I did. The others were under no obligation, not then.

"So what's the plan then?" Kate asked. "Are we going in balls to the wall, or do you have something else in mind?"

We? I don't think so!

I stared at the sea of wilderness. It looked daunting... No, it looked frickin' impossible.

"I'm working on it," I said, more to myself than to anybody else. "I'm working on it," I mused, quietly.

"So, work out loud," Bob said. "You never know, we might be able to provide a little input."

I turned and grinned at him. "Always the blunt one, you are. Okay, so—" At that point, the image froze. The two guards weren't moving.

"What the hell?" I said, turning to Tim.

"We've lost the feed from the satellite; it's passed on and won't be back for another ninety minutes. It's okay though. I recorded it, so I can run what we have on a loop, just give me a minute to set it up." He tapped at the keyboard, then looked up at me and said, "Here you go." He tapped a single key, and the images again lit up both screens.

"Tim," I said. "I need you to record each pass throughout the day. I need to know what's going on up there. And I especially need to know the guard's schedule, if they're on one."

"Gotcha. I'll set that up."

"Great, thanks."

I stepped in as close to the screen as I could, then backed off again, my eyes unfocused.

"Geez," I said. "That's the way to get a headache in a hurry. Okay, so I'm still not sure exactly what that depression here is." I pointed to it. "How deep is it, I wonder? There's no way to tell."

"Yes, there is," Tim said. "Not right now though. This afternoon, say around five o'clock, I might be able to give you some idea. It won't be precise of course, but it will give you a clue."

"You can?" Jacque asked. "And how might you do that?"

Oh no. Now we'll never shut him up.

"Well," Tim said, rising enthusiastically to the occasion, "the depression is almost due east of the compound; the sun sets in the west, so…"

"You'll be able to tell by the density of the shadow," I finished for him.

"Well, yeah, but it's not quite that easy, but in principle, yes. That's basically it."

"You're thinking that if it's deep enough," Kate said, thoughtfully, "we can use it to—"

"Get close enough without being seen to effect a breach in the fence," I finished for her.

"Oh hell, Harry," Bob said, derisively. "You've been watching too many movies. Real life ain't like that. I wish to hell it was."

"You think?" I asked, smiling to myself. I hadn't watched a movie of any kind in more than a year.

I stepped away from Tim's desk and the monitors, sat down, and stared up at them.

"Those cameras," I mused, out loud. "Are they fixed, do you think?"

Tim tapped the keyboard, and the image zoomed so fast it made my head spin. It blurred, stabilized, backed out, refocused on one post and the camera thereon, and we watched. The image was still too small. If the camera was moving, I couldn't tell... not at first, then I blinked, closed my eyes and opened them again. It had moved, at least I thought it had.

"It's programmed, right, Tim?"

"Looks like it. Yeppy. See? It's moving."

We watched. My eyes were straining to see. It didn't look like it was moving to me.

"Come on, Tim," I said. "Talk to me. What are you seeing?"

"It's moving all right, and quite quickly. I make the arc to be about forty-five degrees, maybe fifty. It's taking fifty-five seconds to complete its rotation, each way."

"Oh shit," Bob growled, "Fifty-five seconds? That's no damn good."

"If it's all we have—"

"It's just enough to get us caught," Bob said, interrupting me.

I nodded. "Then we'll just have to be *really* careful," I said, mocking him.

"So that's your plan, then?' he asked. "You're out of your frickin' mind."

"Do you have a better idea?" I asked.

"Yeah, I like bustin' through the gate a whole lot better, or maybe even the fence."

"Now who's been watching too many movies?" I asked, smiling at him.

"Harry," he said. "I'm with you, you know that, but for God's sake... we need a plan, a real, workable plan."

"Like I said," I replied. "Do you have any ideas?"

He stared up at the screen, then, shook his head.

"Okay, then," I said. "We wait until this afternoon, until Tim can give us an idea exactly how deep that depression might be."

I looked around at the group. Most of them had said little, but all had listened intently.

"Okay," I said. "There's little more we can do for now, not until we know the guards' schedule and if the depression is a viable option. If it is, you and I'll go in tonight, Bob, late, around midnight. Any questions, anybody?"

"I do," Kate said. "I'm going with you."

"No!" I said, and I held up my hand to stop her from saying anything. "We'll discuss it later."

She opened her mouth to speak, but I stopped her before she could. "I said, later. Now, if that's it, I'm going to spend a little time with my wife."

I checked my watch. It was just after eleven-thirty.

"I don't want any of you going to the office. Take the rest of the day off. You can stay here. Rose is providing lunch. Get some rest. We'll resume at three o'clock."

I turned to Kate. "I know, but you can't, so drop it. Would you mind taking me to the hospital, please? You can drop me off, and I'll get an Uber to bring me back."

The look she gave me would have frozen a polar bear, but she nodded, and I followed her up the stairs and out to the cars. And there, wouldn't you know it, we found my old friend and Amanda's colleague from Channel 7, Charlie "Pitbull" Grove.

"Hey, Harry," he yelled over the gate. "You took some running down. How about an exclusive, old buddy."

"Charlie, you piece o' shit," I said. "Get the hell away from here and don't tell anyone you know where I am. If you do…" I left the threat unstated.

He looked mortally wounded. Maybe I was a little too hard on him. He was, after all, not as bad as some of the kids the other channels have running around with mikes in their hands.

"But, Harry—"

"No buts, Charlie." But then a thought entered my mind… *Hey, Harry, you could do a whole lot worse than Charlie. At least you can trust him not to bend your words.*

"Look, Charlie, tell you what: I will give you an exclusive, but here's the deal. Right now, I'm up to my eyes in… something. Let me get through it, and we'll sit down and talk. I'll give you all the time you need… well, within reason, but you've got to keep my location to yourself. Deal?"

He thought about it for a minute, then nodded and said, "Deal, but I need for you to throw me a bone."

I was about to stop him, but…

He held up his hand and said, "No, no, no, Harry. Hear me out. I need to know about Amanda. We're all worried sick about her. How is she, Harry?"

I sighed, nodded, and said, "Okay, here's what I know, and it's not much.

I spent the next couple of minutes bringing him up to date—the short version of what had happened—off camera, of course. I left him with a promise that I would call him. He left looking decidedly pleased with himself.

I SPENT the rest of the morning sitting beside Amanda's bed holding her hand, whispering promises I knew I'd probably not be able to keep—but I meant them at the time—and leaving out any mention of what I'd now gotten myself involved in.

What bothered me most about it all was that I made the same promises to myself only a couple of days earlier. *So much for good intentions. Oh well, as Scarlett would say, tomorrow is another day... if I'm lucky.*

Amanda? As far as I could tell, there had been no change. She looked much the same except that the bruises were not quite so dark, and the cuts—held together with butterfly strips—didn't look quite so red. She looked very peaceful, beautiful, and the next thing I knew I was up, on my feet, and out of the room. I was frickin' devastated.

And here I am doing it all again.

I had barely made it through the door into the corridor when I bumped into Dr. Cartwright.

"Hello, Mr. Starke. I was hoping to see you. The front desk told me you were here. You want to know how she is, I suppose. Well, I have some good news for you. First, her condition is stable and improving. We ran an MRI earlier this morning, and the swelling on the right side of her brain is receding quite nicely. I'm going to keep her as-is for the next forty-eight hours and then reassess the situation. If all goes well, and she continues to make progress, I should be able to bring her out of the coma on..." He thought for a moment, then said, "Let's try for Tuesday the 29th. So there, I hope that helps you to feel a little better."

Doc, you have no frickin' idea. You just lifted the Market Street bridge off of my shoulders.

I was so overwhelmed by the good news, I couldn't find the words to thank him. Instead, I grabbed his hand in both of mine and squeezed. I swear the poor man winced.

"Thanks, Doctor," I whispered, barely loud enough for him to hear, then I let go of his hand and, head down, I turned and reentered Amanda's room, sat down beside her, put my face on her stomach and... yeah, I cried. Yeah, that's what I did. I couldn't help it, and you know what, I don't give a damn what you think.

I stayed with her for another hour, then I upped and left to share the good news with August and Rose and... Jade.

It was just after two-thirty that afternoon when the Uber driver dropped me at the gate. I found August in his office, lately vacated by Jacque. He was hunting and pecking on his old desktop PC.

"Harry," he said, looking up as I entered the room. "How is she, son?"

"She's doing fine... Look, where's Rose. I'd like her to hear it too."

"She's in the bedroom, I think, with the baby. Shall we go and see?"

He stood, and I followed him to their master suite where Rose was seated on the bed holding Jade in her arms. She looked, no they looked... lovely together, like they were mother and daughter. I looked at my father, and I could tell he was moved by the scene, but my dear old dad never was one for sentimentalities, not like me, that's for sure.

"Rose," he said, "Harry has good news."

She looked up at me expectantly. I squatted beside her and held out my arms. She handed the baby to me, and I was gifted with a look from Jade's amazing green eyes and... yes, she smiled up at me. Well, I thought she did. Rose told me later it was just gas that made her look like that... but I still wasn't so sure.

While I held Jade, I told Rose and August what the doctor had said.

Much as I wanted to stay with my daughter, I couldn't; I had a lot to do, and quickly if we were going to pull off what I had in mind that evening. So, reluctantly, I handed her back to Rose and headed down to the basement.

13

FRIDAY, MAY 25, 3PM

Riverview
    I checked in with Rose, then headed down to join the others. They were already there and waiting for me when I arrived in the basement: Tim, Kate, Jacque, and Bob.

"Hey, Harry," Tim said as I took my seat. "Did you see Amanda? How is she?"

"She's doing great, Tim. Dr. Cartwright said he hopes to bring her out of the coma on Tuesday, so she's going to make it."

That statement set off a round of conversation that I won't bore you with. Suffice it to say, the mood in the room, including mine, lifted tremendously.

"Okay," I said, finally, "we have work to do. Let's get to it. Before we do, though, Tim, what have you done about upgrading the security?"

"I need to check, but Jack Thomas should be at the office on Georgia Avenue right now. He's scheduled to come here to Riverview tomorrow and your home on Lookout Mountain on Monday."

"Monday's no good, Tim. I need the house done tomorrow. He'll need to split his crew. Tell him I'll pay for the overtime, but make sure he gets it done. Now, let's talk about Copperhill. Bob, what are your thoughts?"

The mood turned serious. Bob thought for a minute, then said, "You sure you want to do this, Harry? We could have the local sheriff go in instead of us."

"That's not an option," I said. "He'd need to get search warrants, and we have no probable cause. Besides, it would take days, and we don't have that kind of time. We can do it."

I thought for a minute, tapped the tabletop with my fingers, then looked and continued, "Look, they won't be expecting us, so we'll have that advantage. If all goes well, we'll be in and out in less than fifteen minutes."

Bob looked at me, skeptically. "Harry you have no idea what we'll be up against, what these people are capable of. They're ex-Rangers, for God's sake."

"Yes, but how many could there be? Tim says most of Christmas' assets are deployed. Look, I'm not planning on starting a war. I've had enough of that to last me the rest of my days. So," I said, "we go in, we grab Joe if he's there, and we get out. It shouldn't be too difficult."

"Harry," Bob said, shaking his head. "You can't be serious. Just the two of us, you and me? We don't have the manpower."

"Three," Kate said. "I'm in."

"The hell you are—"

"Shut up, Harry," she said. "I said I'm in. Joe is my case. I'm in. No arguments."

I shook my head, frustrated. Hell no, more than that. I was scared; I didn't want to put Kate at risk, but knowing her as I did—

"What's the matter, Harry," she asked, with a mocking smile on her lips. "It's easy, right? You just said so. In and out in fifteen minutes, you said. You did mean that, didn't you?"

"Whew," I sighed. "Okay, but you'll do as your damn well told, capiche?"

She nodded, still smiling. Oh yeah, I knew that look, and right then I knew I was wasting my time arguing with her.

"Geez," Bob said. "That's all we need. Okay, but we still don't have enough—"

"How about T.J.?" Kate asked

"Oh no," Jacque said. "Not him, he's crazy, looney toons."

"Kate's right," Bob said. "And so are you, Jacque. Crazy? For sure, but he's just the kind of crazy we need for a job like this. And there's nobody else, so we don't have a choice."

"Perhaps we don't," I said, "but he does. Look, I'll talk to him. If he agrees, he's in." *Ha, that's a joke. He'll agree all right. Jacque is right: the man's a loon.*

"Okay," I said, "if we count T.J. in, that's four—"

"Five," Tim interrupted me.

"Six," Jacque said.

"Oh no, no, no, no," I said. "That's not happening. Tim, you couldn't fight your way out of a wet paper bag, and you..." I paused and glared at Jacque. "Not one chance in hell, young lady."

"Okay," Tim said. "I didn't say I was going into the compound, but you guys can't go in either, not blind. You don't know the territory and—"

"And you do?" I interrupted him. "*No!*"

He grinned happily up at me, stood, and said, "If you'll give me a minute, please?"

Then he went to the door and out to where his van was parked. He opened the rear door of the van, clambered inside, and then backed out again dragging a large and obviously heavy metal case and, using both hands, hauled it inside.

He set it down on the floor and unsnapped the three metal latches, opened the lid, stood upright, and stepped back so that we all could see what was inside.

"Holy crap," I said, looking down at the biggest damn drone I'd ever seen outside of the military. "How the hell much did that cost me? You did it again, you little... I told you to ask before you go spending my money."

He shrugged. "Well, it's a... it's a hexacopter. It's not the most expensive one on the market—the entire package was less than ten thousand—but it does have reasonably good optics. I chose this model because of its extended flight time. I added a couple of upgrades, modified the power supply, basically trading payload for power and endurance. I also added a double gimbal assembly, two extra cameras—night vision and infrared— and I have four extra sets of batteries and one or two other bits and pieces."

I glared at him.

"We had to have one, Harry," he said, plaintively. "And you know only too well, you get what you pay for. This unit is the absolute best choice for what you do—or might do. No self-respecting agency should be without one. Should they?"

I stared at him in wonder. Sometimes the boy was beyond even my comprehension. How many times had I wanted to chastise him? I'd lost count, but it never happened. All it took was a look from those soft, puppy dog eyes and I was lost. But those eyes... Oh, they were so misleading: Tim was a wolf and as crafty as a fox, and my agency was his own personal hen house. That being so, he got away with not quite murder, but close enough. I just shook my head, exasperated.

He got the message, smiled and said, "Good, you see what I mean, right? So I'll be there, in the van, flying the drone. I'll be your eye in the sky. You *will* have to be in and out quickly though. Even with the upgrade, even with *my* upgrades, this baby is good for only about fifty-five minutes of flight time before I have to recharge the batteries or change them."

I looked at Bob, questioningly. He smiled and nodded.

"Okay, you're in, but—" I began.

"An' what about me?" Jacque asked, in full Jamaican mode. "I can help Tim and—"

"Okay, okay," I said, "but only in the van with Tim." *It ain't gonna happen. I'll have to figure out a way to keep her out of it. But keep her out of it I will.*

"Jacque, I need you to call T.J.," I said, "and have him join us."

She nodded, smiling, and headed back up the stairs to make the call. T.J. arrived thirty minutes later.

T.J. Bron is something of an enigma. Only a few months ago, he was on the streets, homeless, and ready to do away with himself. But while he was preparing to off himself, he stumbled upon the body of a young woman in an alley at the rear of the Sorbonne.

Kate was the investigating officer. What she saw in him... ah, who knows. Whatever it was, she took him under her wing and brought him to me. Turns out he's a war hero, a highly decorated Vietnam vet—two tours, the first beginning in 1968 and then again in 1972—an ex-Marine down on his luck...

Nope, luck had nothing to do with it. He was the victim of a shady bank officer who accused him of stealing from the bank: he didn't do it. He did some time, and it ruined him. He lost everything: wife, kids, home. He has a degree in accounting, and at the time, I happened to be looking for a financial investigator. Bearing in mind the man's military record, including his earning of a Silver Star and two Purple Hearts, I figured I could take a chance and hire him. So I did. Jacque found him a place to live, and here we are.

At sixty-eight, T.J. is way older than the rest of my team. However, he's also in way better shape than any of them, perhaps with the exception of Bob and, on a good day, me; this being due to a rigorous workout regimen he started the day Jacque took him in hand and that still continues.

T.J. is six feet, 190 pounds, with white hair and a heavily lined, deeply tanned face. What I didn't know when I hired him was that he's crazy... No, I don't mean he's insane, far from it, but he is absolutely fearless, has a wicked taste for violence, and will kill without hesitation, as I found out only in the last couple of days or so. So yes, I had my doubts about involving him, but I also knew he would be highly pissed off if I didn't.

While we were waiting for him, I spent some time alone, thinking about what I needed to do, trying to formulate a plan. The problem was, as Tim had so rightly pointed out, we didn't know the property or the surrounding terrain. In the end, I decided to keep it simple and go for the direct approach.

So, when T.J. arrived at around four-thirty, we, the six of us, were seated together in a circle around a small card table in the basement. I told him to grab a chair and join us.

"T.J.," I said, "when I hired you, it was never my plan to involve you in what can only be called black ops, but—"

"Yeah?" he said, leaning forward on his chair, his elbows on his knees, his hands clasped together in front of him. He was wearing a black Tee, jeans and Nike sneakers. He was also carrying the VP9 I'd given to him only days before in a holster on his right hip. He looked like an aging gangster, but looks, as they say, can be deceptive.

Anyway, I had his attention.

"Jacque's told you what's happened, to my uncle Joe, right?"

"She did. Someone grabbed him. So, we gonna go get him?"

And there it was. I knew I didn't even need to ask the question, T.J. was in.

"We are, if he's there. We think we know who has him, but where on the property we're not sure. So, we'll just have to cross that bridge when and if we need to."

"Harry," Kate said, quietly. "We have to keep it clean. If we go in there, there can be no killing."

"I told you, Kate: I'm not looking to start a war. All I want is to get Joe out. That's all I want, okay?"

She didn't look okay, but she nodded, and I continued.

"Tim, bring up the satellite images please."

He swiveled his seat to face his array, and we waited while he tapped the keyboard until we had a bird's eye view of the Gypsum Pond area on one of the big monitors.

"Okay, this is the latest recording, right?" I asked.

"Yes," Tim said, checking the time stamp. "It's thirteen minutes ago."

"What about the depression? Any idea how deep it might be?"

"Not really. It's still early, but eighteen inches, maybe two feet. I'll know better when the satellite makes its next pass, in about seventy-five minutes."

Damn, I thought. *It's not deep enough... Sheesh, it will have to be; it's all we've got!*

I looked at my watch, then said, "So, around six o'clock?"

He nodded.

I thought for a minute, then said, "We have to make preparations, so we have to make a decision, now. We'll go tonight, late. I want to be there no earlier than midnight. Tim, you'll take your van and the drone. You can fly that thing, right?"

"Oh... yeah!" He grinned and poked at his glasses.

"At night?"

"Yeppy!"

I shook my head, amazed, and continued, "I'll take Bob, Kate, and T.J. to this point here." I pointed with a pool cue. "Then we'll take this track and park here, in the trees. It's about as close as we can get to the depression without being seen by the cameras, about a hundred feet. There's a camera on the corner, here." I pointed. "We wait for it to make its sweep and turn in the other direction. At that exact moment, we make a run for the depression. We should be able to make it before the camera reverses its sweep. If the depression is deep enough, we should be okay."

I paused, stared at the screen, and then said, "Tim, you'll park somewhere on the road in this area here, out of sight, but somewhere where you can fly that thing."

"Wait," Tim said. "You'll all have body cams and earbuds, so we can see and hear everything you do, and I can communicate with you."

"We?" I said. "You said we."

"Yes," he said. "Me and Jacque. I'm going to need her to monitor the body cams while I fly the drone."

Oh hell, there goes that idea!

I glanced at Jacque. She smiled sweetly at me. *Damn!*

"I'm thinking," I said, "that if we can get to this point here, we can—"

"Okay," Bob interrupted me. "We make it to the trench, then we can what?"

"We blow the fence and head for this building, here. I figure from the vehicles parked outside that it might be the office. We subdue the occupants—there's no point in expecting them to talk. Then... we look for Joe. We grab him and get out of there."

"And that's your plan?" Bob asked, skeptically.

"It is," I snapped, and immediately regretted it. "Look, I don't know what's there any more than you do. We don't have the time or the wherewithal to do a proper recon. We're going to have to play it as we find it. If you have a better idea, I'd like to hear it."

He shook his head. "Nope."

"Okay, I said. "It's now five-thirty-five. We'll meet back here at eight. In the meantime, we'll get something to eat—I think Rose has made sandwiches. Tim, you and Jacque get everything you need together and make sure it's all working, especially the drone. Bob, we'll need weapons, body armor and something to blow the fence. That means a trip to the office. You and Kate can handle that, right?"

He nodded.

"Good," I continued. "There are some half-pound packs of C-4 in the gun room. A couple should be enough... make it four, just in case. T.J., you'll stay here with me. Any questions, anybody? No? Good. Let's go eat."

14

SATURDAY, MAY 26, 12:05AM

C opperhill
By eight o'clock that evening, we were all back together in the basement. By ten, all was ready, except that we still had to get into the body armor.

Bob and Kate had returned loaded with gear, including four Sig Sauer M400 AR15s. *I'm not too sure about letting T.J. loose with one of those,* I thought, *but what the hell... finish what you start, right?*

They also brought just about every handgun we owned and enough ammunition to start a small war. Bob never did anything by halves.

I donned my lightweight, Tactical Scorpion vest—ceramic plates front and back—my VP9 in a holster on my right hip along with three extra mags, plus two more for AR, Tim's body cam and earbuds, and I was ready to go.

I looked at my companions: Bob and Kate's faces were devoid of expression; T.J., however, was grinning.

He looked like a frickin' crocodile about to devour a duck. *Oh hell,* I thought, *I really don't know about this.*

I turned to Tim. "You ready, son?"

He looked pale, but he nodded.

"Jacque, you sure about this?"

She also nodded, a determined look on her face.

"Kate... you're sure you want to do this?"

She nodded, grimly, looking like a real badass in her tactical gear and with an AR tucked under her arm.

"Okay," I said, turning to the already open door where Bob had parked his Hummer alongside Tim's van. "Let's go."

WE ARRIVED at the first waypoint on Highway 64 at eleven-fifty and turned left onto what must have once been a mine access road. It was still in good condition, which meant it was still in use, probably by CSC. We would leave Tim and Jacque parked just off the road under cover of some trees, and we waited while Tim opened the rear doors of his van, readied the drone, checked all of the monitors to make sure we were all in communication, and then he launched the drone. I was surprised by how quiet it was. The six lifters whispered as the machine left the ground and rose quickly until I could no longer see it.

I watched Tim as he operated the controls. He looked up at me, a huge smile lighting up his face, then he gave me a thumbs up, climbed back into the van and closed the doors.

"Sound and video check, please," I heard Tim say through the earbuds.

One by one, we checked in, then Tim said, "Okay, you're fit to go. I have video feed from the drone. You want to see?"

"Yes, but we don't have time—fifty-five minutes, didn't you say?"

"Right. You should go. The drone should be over the compound in three minutes. Harry, let me know when you're in position. Well, you don't really need to. I'll be able to see you, but—"

"I'll check in, Tim," I said, dryly, interrupting him.

Five minutes later, we were out of the Hummer and lying prone under the trees at the edge of the open space in front of the compound and... damn it, I couldn't see the depression. Which really wasn't surprising, because Tim had estimated it to be two feet deep at best, and some six feet wide.

"Tim, are you receiving me?" I whispered.

"Yup, and I see all four of your heat signatures. I can also see a lot of signatures in three of the six buildings. I estimate at least sixty, maybe seventy occupants, most of them in the big building."

"Holy cow," Bob said. "Are you serious?"

"I am. Are you still a go?"

I looked sideways at them; they all three nodded. Bob and Kate were grim. T.J. had his teeth bared, his eyes half-closed; it was a look of total concentration. *Geez, he's a scary looking bastard.*

"Yeah, we're still a go," I said. "Where the hell is that trench?"

"It's to your right. You should be able to see the corner light post from where you are. Can you?"

"Yes, I see it."

"Okay, you need to head for that. I timed the camera. It's on a fifty-second sweep cycle, a little less than I'd hoped, but you can make it. On my mark. Get ready... Okay, go, go, go."

And we upped, and we ran. It was the longest hundred and sixty feet of my life, but we made it, just in time.

I threw myself into the trench—it was indeed about six feet wide but a little deeper than Tim's estimate, maybe thirty inches; maybe a little less, but better than I'd hoped. Kate landed on top of me, Bob a dozen feet further back, and T.J., wouldn't you know it, was fifteen feet closer to the fence than I was.

"Okay, okay," I heard Tim in my ear. "I see you. Get down, *now!* Okay, it's swinging back again. What's the plan now?"

"Tim, and the rest of you," I said, "listen up. Tim, I need you to watch the camera. Give me the word, and I'll make a run for the light post. If I can get there without being seen, I should be out of the camera's sightline. I'll set a charge and bring the post down; the camera and the fence will come down with it, I hope. We'll head for the nearest building and gain access. Then hell, who knows? T.J., for God's sake, no shooting unless..." *Oh, hell. What's the use?*

"T.J.," I said. "You hear me? Answer me, damn it."

"Take it easy, boss. I hear you. No shooting unless... Don't worry, I got it, and your back."

It wasn't much, but I had to live with it.

"Okay, Tim," I said. "What about the guards?"

"I don't see any. You ready, Harry? On my mark... *Go!*"

I jumped out of the trench and ran for the post and dropped to the floor at its base. It was round, made of steel, hollow, I hoped, and the fence—horizontal steel bars with thick steel wire net between them—was anchored to it on both sides. Beyond that, maybe seventy-five feet away was the nearest of the six buildings. It still figured it might be an office, but the side and rear that I could see had no windows or doors.

I looked at the light pole, shook my head, and wondered, *Geez, it's too fricking big. A half-pound might not be enough. Better use two.*

"*Harry!*" Tim yelled in my ear. "*Get down.* Someone's just exited the building and is coming toward you."

Holy shit! There was no cover. What could I do? I dropped flat on my face, my hand on my VP9, and I lay still, waited, and watched.

He came into sight, walking slowly. He was wearing combat camo and carrying what looked like an assault rifle. *One of the guards.*

I eased the VP9 out of its holster, took a deep breath, and steeled myself for what I was sure was about to come: it didn't. He stopped, stood for a moment, looked around, let the rifle hang from its sling, and lit a cigarette, and then turned and slowly walked back out of sight. *Whew!*

I lay still for several moments, barely breathing. Then I rolled over onto my back, slipped the VP9 into its holster, and removed two half-pound slabs of C-4 from the pockets of the jacket I was wearing over my vest, and set them to the base of the pole. I wired them together with an electronic detonator and waited for Tim to give me the word. A couple of minutes later, I was back in the trench with the others.

"Ready?" I asked, looking round at them. They all nodded. "Tim, how many are there inside that building?"

"Four, that I can see."

"Right," I said. "The fence comes down, and we hit that building, hard. Got it?"

They had. I took a deep breath.

I pushed the trigger and the world ended, or so it seemed at the time, so loud was the explosion the ground shook. In fact, what happened was: the two packs of C-4 sheered the pole at its base, bringing it down along with the camera and at least fifty feet of steel fence. *Hmm, a half-pound would have been plenty after all.*

"*Let's go!*" I shouted and jumped to my feet, running as hard as I could go for the front of the building. I covered the distance in no more than ten seconds, maybe less. Even so, I barely made it before the door opened. I slammed into it without stopping, blasting it wide open, smashing it into the two guards that were about to exit.

I careened on through the doorway, almost falling over one of the guards; Bob was right on my ass, followed by... No, not T.J., by Kate.

"*Drop your weapons!*" I shouted at the two men still on their feet, my AR at the ready. They were taken completely by surprise. For a few seconds, they stood as if they were frozen, then their weapons clattered onto the concrete floor.

"*Good,*" I was still shouting. "*Now, get down, on the floor, quickly, and stay still, all of you.*" And, slowly, the two men, never taking their eyes off me, lowered themselves to join the other two. *Sheesh, so far so good.*

"Bob," I said, "strap 'em up. Kate, you and T.J. head for that next building and see what you can find, and for God's sake be careful, especially you." I glared at T.J.; he grinned back at me, and they took off.

"Tim, give Kate and T.J. a heads-up, okay?"

He said he would, and I heard him giving them directions.

"There are four people in there. Wait, wait... T.J., two just exited at the front and are heading your way, running. *Watch out. They're almost on top of you.*"

I waited, listening. Neither T.J. nor Kate answered. Then I heard a volley of automatic fire, followed by the steady pop-pop-pop of an AR15 and the heavier bam-bam-bam of a handgun.

"Oh shit, Kate. What's happening. Answer me damn it."

"It's okay," she came back. "We have it under control. They're both down."

"Oh shit," I yelled. "Are they dead?"

"No. Not yet anyway. T.J. clipped one in the arm; he went down. He's yelling like an idiot, the guard is, not T.J. The other guy fell over him and hit his head. He's out cold. We're about to enter the building. You all okay?"

I told her I was, and then while I kept our four guards at gunpoint, Bob strapped them up with heavy cable ties. That done, I sat on the desk and looked down at them.

"Harry," Tim said. "You have twenty minutes more

before I have to recall the drone. How much longer are you going to be?"

"Hell, I don't know. Do what you gotta do, Tim. We'll cope."

I turned my attention to the guards.

"Which one of you is in charge?" I asked.

No one answered.

I sighed, shook my head, and said, "Okay, if that's the way you want to play it. I'll ask one more time. If I don't get an answer, one of you will lose your balls. Now, who's in charge?"

"He is." It was the smallest of the four who answered.

"You?" I said, leaning forward. "You're holding a friend of mine, a man, an older man with special needs. I want him. Where is he?"

"I don't know."

I slammed the barrel of the AR15 down on his knee cap as hard as I could. I heard the cap crack, and he howled like a wolf in the night, and then he passed out. *Damn!*

"Now," I said, quietly. "Who wants to go next? Come on, one of you, answer me. I don't have all night."

I looked at the small guy, the one who'd given up his boss.

"You," I said, "where is he?"

"He—there ain't—"

I slammed the gun down on his knee. I almost missed; clipped the side of it.

"Ow, oh God. Oh, ow."

I shoved the muzzle of the gun hard into his package.

"Oof! Screw you."

I nodded, removed the mag from the AR, cleared the chamber, reinserted the mag and slowly eased back the bolt until it cocked and locked, and let it slam back into position, loading a new round into the chamber.

Again, I stabbed the muzzle into his package, my finger on the trigger, and I looked into his eyes, my eyebrows raised; the question was plain enough.

"Go to hell!"

I nodded, looked him in the eye and said, "The magic number is three," and I began to count: "One... two..."

He closed his eyes and, for a moment, I thought he was going to tough it out, but he didn't.

"He's in the next building. There's a room at the back."

"Kate, can you hear me. Joe's in your building—in a room at the back."

"Okay, I hear you."

"Okay, we're heading your way," I said.

I looked down at my four prisoners. They weren't going anywhere.

"Let's go," I said to Bob, and I ducked out of the door; Bob followed.

"Harry," Tim said in my ear. "Someone needs to take a look in that big building. There are a lot of heat signatures."

"Okay, but we have to get Joe out of here first."

By the time we arrived, Kate had already found Joe. They had him locked in a small—no tiny—room at the back of the second building. T.J. had overpowered the third guard, and Kate had smashed the flimsy lock with the butt of her AR.

The main door into the building was wide open, and T.J. was just inside holding three guards at gunpoint. Two of them, a guy with a knot on his head the size of an egg, and a young woman aged about twenty-five, were on the floor with their hands strapped together behind their backs. A third man was lying against the wall in a corner of the room. His face the color of dirty rice, he was holding his arm, trying to stop the blood leaking out between his fingers. An Israeli Tavor assault rifle lay on a table close to where T.J. was standing, along with another fully automatic rifle, two 10mm Glock 29s, a Glock 17, and a Glock 43, which I assumed must belong to the woman.

I left Bob with T.J. and joined Kate in the back room where she was trying to sooth an extremely upset Joe. He was shaking like a leaf and tears were streaming down his cheeks.

"Harry," he yelled and jumped to his feet and flung his arms around my neck. "They were mean to me, Harry. They said they were going to do bad things to me. They said they were going to cut my pecker off. You won't let them cut it off, will you, Harry?" he sobbed.

"Hush, Joe," I said, holding him tight. "I'm here now. No one's going to hurt you, I promise. Now calm down. We're going to get you out of here.

"I'm scared, Harry. Please don't let them cut me."

"I won't let them cut you. Now let's get out of here."

I let go of him, turned him around, put my arm around his shoulder, and steered him out into the larger room.

"It was him," Joe said, pointing to the guard lying in

the corner. "He was going to cut my pecker off. He said so, lots of times."

"It's okay, Joe," I said. "He's not going to cut anybody. Now look, I need for you to help me. I need for you to do exactly what I tell you. Will you do that for me?"

He nodded, tearfully.

"Listen to me very carefully. T.J. here, is going to take you to my car where you and he will wait for me, okay?"

"No, no, no, Harry. I want you to stay with me, pleeease!"

"Joe, listen to me. I'll only be a couple of minutes, but I have to do this. You're safe now. Go with T.J. to the car. I think there's some candy in the glove box."

At that, he brightened up a little but was still reluctant to leave me.

T.J., however, much to my surprise, took his hand and said, "C'mon, Joe. Let's get that candy before the others steal it all."

And that was all it took. T.J. led him off into the night.

"Harry," Kate said. "Over there."

I looked at where she was pointing. The building was bigger than I'd first thought, maybe fifty by thirty. On the far side, two rows of trestle tables, two of which were piled high with plastic-wrapped packages. On the second row of tables were several dozen plastic trays, two sets of scales, and a small wrapping machine. We were in a damned illegal drug factory.

"Shit," Bob said, "I knew it. That son of a bitch is importing drugs for distribution. I'm gonna frickin' burn it—"

"No," I said, interrupting him. "We'll leave it for the law."

"The law," he almost exploded. "This is government property, remember? No, Harry, this is my call. Get the hell out of here and let me do what I gotta do."

I hesitated. *Aw, what the hell do I care?* I thought. *If we leave it... who knows what will happen to it. If they were able to get the word out that we were here, Christmas' men might already be on their way.*

"Okay, do it. There's a fuel tank with a pump on it outside, to the left, between the two buildings. Make sure you get them safely out first." I nodded at the three guards. "We'll go and see what the hell they're up to in that other building."

So I left him to it, and Kate and I exited the building and headed north toward what looked like a small, commercial chicken rearing house.

The main door was at the center of the building. It was locked; a padlock through a hasp on the outside. From what I could see, I figured it was there more to keep people in, rather than out. One hard kick and the hasp tore out of the frame.

We stepped back, guns at the ready, and waited: nothing. I stepped forward and cautiously eased the door outward and open. I held my breath, listened, still nothing, then: *Was that a whimper?*

Yes, that's what it was.

We stepped inside, and I got the shock of my life. In both directions, the far wall was lined with cages. There had to be at least fifty of them. The interior was lit with a string of tungsten light bulbs, each about twenty feet apart, that stretched all the way down the center of the building from one end to the other. In the dim light, it was just possible to see that some of the cages were occupied: mostly women of varying ages, some Asian, some Hispanic, some as young as eight or ten. I didn't count them, but I estimated there were at least fifty, with room enough for three times that number.

And then they started to shout and scream.

"Oh, my, God," Kate whispered. "What the hell is this place?"

"Looks like they're into trafficking as well as drugs," I said. "Now we don't have a choice. We have to call the authorities. Go stop Bob from firing that building."

But it was too late, just as she stepped out of the door, there was a loud whoosh and then an explosion as the windows blew out of the building.

"Tim," I said. "You there?"

"I'm here, Harry. I had to pull the drone. It was running out of power. What do you need?"

"I need you to give us time to get clear, then call the local sheriff's department and get them up here. There are at least fifty women and kids caged in that main building. Use a burner phone, and don't for God's sake let 'em know who we are. Understand? Good. Have T.J. and Joe got there yet? They have? Good. Wrap things up and make ready to get out of there. Give us fifteen minutes. If we're not there by then, make the call, and go. No ifs or buts. You make the call. You understand?"

"But, Harry—"

"Damn it, Tim. Do as you're frickin' told, just once, will you?'

He said he would, and I went after Kate. I found them together, standing over the three prisoners. Bob had dragged them out into the open—watching the building burn.

"Hey," I said. "Get a grip. This ain't the 4th of July. Bob, those three are okay, so let's go check on the four guards in the first building and then get the hell out of here."

Tim was still waiting for us when we arrived. I should have kicked his ass for disobeying me, but he hit me with those big puppy dog eyes, and I didn't have the heart. Besides, we needed to get out of there, and fast, and we did, making it back to Riverview without incident.

MAY 26, 3AM

Riverview

As I said, we made the journey back to Riverview without incident. Joe fell asleep in the back of the Hummer. He didn't wake until I eased him out of the car; that was at just after three o'clock that morning.

We'd been on the road for maybe thirty minutes when I suddenly had a thought, *I haven't seen any first responders... Hell, I haven't even heard any sirens...*

"Bob," I said. "Stop the car. I need to talk to Tim."

He pulled the Hummer off the road; Tim pulled in behind us.

I exited the vehicle and walked back to the van, signaling for him to roll down the window.

"You didn't make the call, did you?" I asked.

"Call? What call—"

"911," I said, interrupting him, shaking my head. "Make it now, airhead. Do it now, and then toss the phone."

"What was that about?" Bob asked, shifting into drive.

"Just Tim being Tim," I said.

AUGUST AND ROSE were at the front door, waiting. No, I'm not going into the reunion, or August's effusive stream of thanks and appreciation to my team and me. Let's just say it was something of a tearjerker. Even T.J. looked a little affected. Anyway, some fifteen minutes after we arrived, Rose had him, Joe, tucked safely in bed in one of the spare rooms.

The rest of us? We arranged to meet at nine the following morning and, with the exception of T.J., who hit the couch, they all went home; Bob providing transport for Kate.

Me? Rose wouldn't let me visit Jade, so I too went to bed, but sleep didn't come easy. Once again, the demons of the night haunted the dark corners of my bedroom. Sleep did come, eventually, but it was restless, fraught with dreams, not quite nightmares, but disturbing, nonetheless.

I woke the following morning, at just after seven, feeling like I'd just run a marathon. I lay there for a minute, staring at the ceiling, breathing deeply, hoping... what? Damned if I could remember, so I rolled out of bed and went out through the sliding glass doors, straight to the pool, dived in and swam laps for the next twenty minutes. Ten more minutes and a quick shower later, I was feeling better than I had for more than a week. We had Joe back, and Amanda was improving. But something I couldn't quite get a grip on was niggling inside my head.

Rose was already up and about, and so was Joe.

I sat down at the kitchen table, and Rose handed me a huge mug of steaming coffee. August was nowhere to be seen. Joe, seemingly without a care in the world, was calmly eating a bowl of cereal.

I sat quietly for a minute, enjoying that first cup of the day, when I remembered that T.J. was in the living room

I poured coffee and took it to him. He wasn't there; his clothes were. *What the hell?*

"Hey, Harry. Hope you slept as well as I did."

I turned and stared at him.

He was coming in through the door wearing a towel wrapped around his waist, another in his hands toweling at his head. *Geez, the man's built like a weightlifter.*

"So," he said. "I hope you don't mind. I heard you in the kitchen, so I grabbed a shower in your bathroom, and boy did I need it. I was stinkin', Harry. Listen, I got to go get a change of clothes. I'll be back by nine, all right?"

I nodded, realized I was still holding his coffee, and said, "Sure. You want this before you go?"

"Oh yeah. Gimme."

He took it from me and swallowed half of it in a single gulp, then set the mug on the coffee table, dropping the towel from around his waist. You can believe me when I tell you he really was well built. *Time I wasn't here.*

"Okay, T.J., I'll see you back here at nine. Wait a minute—what's that?"

He looked down at his genitals. "What the hell do you think it is?"

"Damn it, TJ., not your dick, you idiot, that cut on your thigh?"

"Oh, that. It's nothing."

"It doesn't look like nothing to me. It looks like a damn bullet crease. Were you hit?"

"I told you. It's nothing. Just a clip, is all. That damned guard got lucky, or not, before I put him down. I never even felt it. I washed it good and soused it with Neosporin. It'll be gone in a couple of days... And talkin' about the guard I shot, you'll note that I did as you asked. I didn't kill him. I should have, but I didn't. Ah, you worry too much, Harry. Now get outa here and let me get dressed."

"You should have told me," I said, but I did as he asked and headed back to the kitchen and more coffee... and eggs and bacon... and toast.

I ate the breakfast and decided to spend what little time was left before the team arrived out on the patio where I could think. I hadn't been there more than ten minutes when August appeared.

"Harry, do you mind if I join you?"

"No, not at all."

He sat down on the bench beside me, put his hand on my knee and, for a moment, said nothing; he just sat and stared at the pool. Me? I just let him be.

"Harry," he said, finally. "You know I can never thank you enough for what you did."

"Stop it, Dad. It's not necessary." Dad? I didn't call him that very often, but somehow it just seemed right.

He squeezed my knee. "Yes, it is, but I know how you are, and I won't embarrass you further. Just know that... I love you, son."

Now that was a rare one and a huge surprise. August wasn't one for endearments.

"I know," I said. "I love you too. Okay, now that we've gotten that out of the way, I can tell there's something on your mind. What is it?"

He was silent for a minute, then said, "It's not over, is it?"

I knew exactly what he meant. "No, probably not."

"So, where do we go from here?"

"We sit tight, and wait," I said. "We have what we wanted. Christmas doesn't, and he's lost his bargaining chip. You haven't dropped the suit and, if I know you, you won't. So, he'll figure out some other way to apply pressure. And there's something else: last night, we destroyed several million dollars' worth of drugs. You can bet he'll be looking for payback for that too... It's not over."

"So that's it? We just sit around and wait."

I nodded. "That's all we can do. It's his move."

We sat for several minutes more, discussing hypothetical scenarios and even more hypothetical options. Yes, it was a waste of time, but I think it helped my father; not a lot, but some.

It was at that point Joe decided to join us.

"Hi Harry," he said, parking himself happily down beside his brother.

"Hi Joe," I replied. "How are you feeling today?"

"I feel good, Harry. And thank you for not letting that man cut off my pecker."

Oh shit, now that's really funny. Just look at August's face.

"You're welcome, Joe," I said.

I couldn't help but smile. August, however, wasn't smiling at all. He was aghast.

"Would you like to explain?" he asked.

And I did.

"Oh, my God," he said, quietly. "What are we dealing with?"

"Good question," I said. "I think we'll know soon enough.

"Augi," Joe said. "I want to see my friends. Can I go home, please?"

"THOSE GUYS WERE NOT RANGERS, HARRY," Bob said.

It was already after ten in the morning and we, the six of us, had been discussing the events of the previous evening for more than an hour.

"It was too easy," Bob continued. "They gave up too easily. Rangers never give up, not while they're still breathing."

"If they weren't Rangers, then what?" I asked.

"I'd say they were new recruits." He paused, then continued, "Probably ex-military. Army, maybe, but not special forces, and certainly not Rangers. And there were only what, seven of them? I always figured Nick was into drugs, but trafficking, that's something I wouldn't have thought he would do." He paused, thought for a minute, then said, "I wonder if that's what Walker was carrying in that box van. If it was, he's sure getting cocky in his old age, is our Nick."

"Okay, that aside, you know the man," I said. "What do you think his next move will be?"

He didn't need to think about it; he already had.

"With Joe now out of his clutches," he said, "Christmas has lost his leverage, so now he has only one option: he has to go after the principal, August. The only way to stop August is to kill him, and Nick won't hesitate to do just that. I'd say he'll come after us, hard, in force, and not with recruits. We can expect the real deal, and sooner rather than later."

I looked around the group. With one exception the expressions on their faces were serious. The exception? I don't need to tell you. T.J. was sitting comfortably, leaning back in his chair, arms folded, a half-smile on his lips.

I can't let them do this, I thought. *Someone's going to die, and I can't let it be one of them.*

"Okay," I said, in a tone that I hoped brooked no arguments. "You guys go home. It's over for you... No, don't. I've seen enough death these last couple of years. I'm not going to lose any of you. Go. I said go... *Now!*"

They didn't move, not one of them. All five of them just continued to sit there, staring at me, unblinking. *Ahhh shit!*

"Come on, guys," I said, softly. "You know I can't let you do this."

"It don't look like you have much say in it, boss," T.J. said. "I know that I, for one, am in it to the end. I owe you, but that aside, I ain't had this much fun since I left Nam."

"These are not gang-bangers we'll be dealing with," I said. "Christmas will send professional soldiers, Army Rangers, for God's sake. We can't fight that kind of power. There aren't enough of us, and we're not trained for it. You could die, all of you."

I paused, waited for someone to say something. No one did.

"T.J.?" I asked.

"Like I told you, boss. I'm stayin'."

"Kate?" I asked, already knowing the answer.

She merely nodded.

I sighed. "Bob?"

"You need to ask?"

"No," I said, quietly. "Jacque?"

"Yes. You know it."

I looked at Tim. He grinned back at me, pushed his glasses further up the bridge of his nose, and nodded enthusiastically.

"I can't let you do it, Tim," I said.

"Ah, but you have to. You need me," he said. "Information is your best weapon, without it, you're blind. You can try and keep me out, but you know I rarely ever take any notice of anything you say. You've told me so yourself, many times. So, you might as well give it up. Like it or not, I'm in."

I looked at each one of them in turn. I couldn't believe that these people would so willingly put their lives on the line for me. Suddenly, I was more choked up than I had ever been, even at Amanda's bedside. *Oh crap. What the hell do I do now?*

I pursed my lips, trying not to show any emotion, then said in a voice that I know must have betrayed me, "So, that's it then, you're sure?"

They all nodded.

I nodded, bit my bottom lip, sucked on it, closed my eyes, thought, made up my mind and said, "Okay then. Now we wait. The ball is now, as they say, in Nick Christmas' court. We can't do anything until we know which way he'll jump."

"We can't do that, Harry," Bob said. "If I know Nick, he'll come in quick and hot, no warning."

"Bob," I said. "I hope to hell you're wrong."

Fortunately, he was. At noon precisely, just as we all sat down to eat lunch, August's phone began to vibrate on the tabletop.

He picked it up, looked at the screen, then at me and said, "No caller ID."

"Answer it. Put it on speaker. Tim, go do your thing. I want to know who it is and where he is."

Tim jumped up and ran to the stairs. August answered the phone.

"Hello."

"Well played, August, or should I say Harry?" the voice was heavily distorted.

Nobody said a word, we all waited.

"Cat got your tongue, August?"

"What do you want, Christmas?" August asked.

"Christmas? What are you talking about? No, I don't want Christmas. What I do want is for you to drop the lawsuit against CSC... Oh, that Christmas. Hahaha. You think this is Nick. He has nothing to do with this. Think again, August."

"No, you think again, whoever you are," August said. "I will not drop the suit."

"Oh, now that's really too bad. I was hoping we could end this thing amicably, but it seems you're not willing to cooperate. Well, I'd like you to take a minute and think about it, and to reconsider. You can't win, August. You can die for what you think is right, and so can your loved ones, but you can't win. I will win. I always do."

"Go to hell," August said.

"Now that really wasn't nice, August. Do you have me on speaker? Yes, of course you do. How's your wife doing, Harry? She's in Erlanger, I believe. Room 3007, as I recall."

My blood ran cold.

"Harry?" he said. "Are you there? Haha, yes, of course you are. I do hope she's feeling better. *August*," the voice hardened, "drop it. Do it today. You have twenty-four hours. If you don't, a lot of people are going to get hurt. And you? Well, that won't matter, because you won't be around to settle the suit, much less take it to trial."

The phone went dead.

The room was quiet. We all just sat there, staring at the silent phone on the table.

"So," I said, finally breaking the silence. "Now we

know. Bob, you think that was Christmas, or are we dealing with someone else, someone he's working for?"

"It was him all right," Bob said. "He was just covering his ass. Harry, we're in serious trouble. He just threatened your entire family. August, I know you don't—"

"Forget it, Bob," August said.

Bob nodded and looked at me.

I shook my head, resignedly. Bob just shrugged.

It was at that moment that Tim came bounding into the room, "Hey, y'all, I got him, but it will do you no good. It was a burner. When he hung up, I lost it. He must have removed and destroyed the chip. Harry, he was less than a quarter mile away on Hixson Pike."

I was stunned, but on thinking about it, I wasn't really surprised. If it were me, that's exactly what I would have done: fear is a great motivator.

"I don't suppose there's any point going after him, is there?" Kate said, then answered her own question. "No, I suppose not. We don't even know what we're looking for. He's long gone."

"So, what do we do now?" Jacque sounded worried.

"You do what Harry said," August said, "and go home. You heard what Christmas—if that's who it was— said. People will die."

"Yeah," T.J. said, "they sure as hell will."

"Not on my account," August said.

"So, you'll drop it, then?" I asked.

He glared at me. "No!"

I shook my head. "Okay, August's right. It's over. Go home. Now!"

No one moved.

"Oh, for God's sake, people," I said. "This isn't a game. We cannot, can't possibly go up against a small frickin' professional army. I'll get August, Rose and the baby out of here, out of the country, right now, today. August, call the airport and have Tom ready the plane, then you and Rose—"

"Stop it, Harry," August said, quietly. "I'm not running, not this time. Rose and the baby, yes, but I'm staying to see this thing through."

Or not, I thought.

"I'll call Tom and tell him Rose and the baby will be there within the hour, but that's it."

"Oh no," Rose said. "If you're staying, so am I."

"*No!*" August snapped, in a voice that brooked no argument. "You have to take the baby to safety."

She looked miserable, and I thought for a minute she was going to argue, but she didn't.

"But where will we go?" she asked.

"Calypso Cay. I'll call Leo and tell him you're coming. Now go and get ready. I want you out of here as soon as possible."

He paused, watched her go, and then turned to me and said, "Now you, Harry."

"Forget it," I said. "I'm staying."

"Yeah, don't even think about it, August," Bob said. "I'm staying too. What's the plan?"

"*Stop!*" August was livid. "What about Amanda? Have you forgotten about her? What if they decide to go after her?"

Oh, God... Yes, in the heat of the moment, I had forgotten about her. *Oh shit, How could I... What the hell do I do now?*

"Put me through to Chief Johnston, please, Kelly."

I looked at Kate. "What the hell are you doing?" I asked her.

She held up her hand. I waited, listening, as she continued.

"Chief, it's me, Gazzara. I need you to put a round-the-clock guard on... Stop, Chief. Give me a fricking minute and I'll tell you. What? Yes, at Erlanger, Harry's wife. Two officers at all times, twenty-four-seven until further notice. Yes, yes, I know, damn it. Harry will pay the overtime. Here, you want to talk to him? No... No... Yes, she's in danger... Right, room 3007. No, Chief, I can't explain, not now. I don't have time. Look, just do it, damn it... Okay... No, I shouldn't, sorry. Later? Yes, I will. I promise."

She looked sheepishly across the kitchen table at me, smiled and said, "Well, after that I guess I just kissed my career goodbye. Two officers are on their way to Erlanger now. Ten minutes, no more."

I didn't know what to say. I just looked at her stunned. She smiled at me, raised her eyebrows, and cocked her head to one side, but she didn't speak. I didn't either, but she knew.

I put my elbows on the table, my head in my hands, and I prayed, something I didn't do very often.

"Okay," Bob said, interrupting my thoughts. "That's Amanda, Rose, and Jade safe. Now what?"

I looked up and said, "Beats me. I need a break. I need to think. In the meantime, I'm open to ideas."

And I rose from the table and went outside, sat down

on a bench poolside, and tried to clear my head. It didn't happen.

I need to see Amanda. Can't... But I might not ever get to again. Bullshit, Harry. Course you will.

16

MAY 26, NOON

Riverview
When I returned to the kitchen some fifteen minutes later, I immediately noticed that T.J. was missing.

"Where'd T.J. go?" I asked as I resumed my seat.

"Don't know," Jacque said. "He said he had something he needed to do, and that he'd be back. He didn't say when."

I nodded. "No problem. Maybe he won't come back. I wish he wouldn't. No, no I don't. He's right, we need him."

I paused and thought for a minute. "Okay, so does anyone have anything to say?"

They didn't, so I continued, "Jacque, the first thing we need to do is close the office. Call and tell them all to go home, indefinitely. Don't tell them why. Just tell them also that you'll pay everyone for the time off. Call it extra —no, call it bonus vacation time."

Jacque jotted on her tablet and then nodded at me.

"Look," I said, "I figure there's no point in trying to hide from this. It would be a waste of time and accomplish nothing. We have to face this thing head-on, but not here. That would be disastrous."

"Harry," Kate said. "Don't you think we should bring in the authorities and let them handle it? They're way better equipped than we are, and—"

"Handle what?" I asked, irritably; she'd ruined my train of thought. "What would you tell them, Kate? Even we don't know that?"

"But the people up there at Copperhill—"

"We weren't there, remember? And we were on government property, and how would we explain the wounded—"

"Harry," Tim raised his hand.

"*What?*" I snapped at him. "Geez, sorry, Tim. What?"

"They weren't there either," Tim said.

"What? What are you talking about?"

"The wounded, the women. Sorry, Harry. I would have told you before, but I got kinda sidetracked."

He looked at Jacque and shrugged. She nodded like she was telling him to go ahead.

"See," he said. "I had my police scanner on. It's something I like to do. Listen in, you know. Sometimes you hear interesting—"

"For God's sake, Tim," I said, "Stop rambling and get on with it."

"The sheriff's officers didn't find anything. By the

time the first responders arrived, it was more than ninety minutes after we left—and that was my fault," he said, looking at me. "I forgot to call... Well, anyway, by the time they got there, the fire was out—nothing left but a pile of ashes, most of that already blown away—you must have used a lot of gas, Bob—and there was no one there... just two guards, which means they must have taken the women and kids away... somewhere... in that box van, I guess."

He caught the look I was giving him and hurriedly continued, "Anyway, they were all gone, all but the two guards in the office. They told the officers the fire was an accident, and that everything was under control, so they left, the officers did. Those folks up there are pretty laid back. I heard one deputy say they'd check in with the owners—I guess that would be CSC—and they left. Sorry."

"You knew all this, Jacque?" I asked, stunned that she hadn't told me. "Why didn't you tell me?"

"I told him not to tell you," she said. "You already have too much on your mind, and I didn't think it would matter anyway, and it doesn't. Not now." She stared at me, defiantly.

"Okay, then," I said, shaking my head, "I guess that answers that question, right, Kate?"

She shook her head, then said, "I guess, but something doesn't add up. We'll deal with that later. Just get on with it."

I nodded. "As I said, we need to face this thing head-on. He, Christmas, won't be expecting that. But not here.

I have a cabin in the mountains, north Georgia. That's where we'll go."

Sheesh, I thought *I haven't been up there since...* Well, that's a whole nother story.

"And do what?" Bob asked. "I thought you said you wanted to face him head-on. How the hell will he know where we are?"

"Tim?" I asked.

He grinned and said, "Cell phone tracking."

"He's too smart for that," Bob said. "He won't fall for it."

"Yes, he will, if you turn 'em off. He'll think you don't know that they can still be tracked. I betcha he'll go for it... Wait a minute... He was here, or someone was, at least they were on Hixson Pike... Why? He could have made that call from Atlanta."

He jumped up and ran out of the house. *What the hell?*

He returned almost immediately, a huge grin splitting his face. He held up a small black box between his finger and thumb.

"GPS tracker," he said, "on the Hummer. I didn't look, but I bet the other vehicles have them too. Christmas could have had a lackey stick the trackers on the cars any time we weren't with the vehicles. So if we turn the phones off, but leave the trackers, they'll know where we are. Easy peasy."

"It makes sense," Bob said. "It's exactly what I would have done."

I nodded, slowly, and sat for a minute, thinking, my head full of all kinds of garbage, then I looked up and said, "Okay, let's get moving. We need to get out of here. Where the hell is T.J.?"

And that's when he walked in followed by two of the roughest, ugliest, scruffiest individuals I have ever seen outside of a soup kitchen, which is exactly where he'd found them.

17

SATURDAY, MAY 26, 1:30PM

Planning the Coup.

"T.J.?" I looked at him quizzically through narrowed eyes. "You want to explain what these two are doing here?"

"No prob', chief. I figured we need some extra help. This is it. Monty, Chuck, say hello to Harry Starke."

I stared at him, then at the two men; they both grinned back at me and said "Hi."

I grabbed him by the arm. "Come with me. You two stay here while I sort this out."

I walked him out of the door into the foyer, turned him around, and said, "Are you out of your cotton-pickin' mind? Where did you find them, at the homeless shelter?"

"Well, seein' as you guessed, yessir, that's where they came from, only I didn't find them. I already knew where they were. They're old friends, buddies from Nam. They don't come any better'n them. I told 'em you'd make it worth their while. When I told 'em what was happenin', they jumped at it. I told them you'd tip 'em a couple of hundred for a couple of days. That was okay, right?"

I was speechless. No, I was dumbfounded.

"No, T.J., it's not going to happen. Geez, the small guy, Monty is his name? He must be seventy-five years old."

"Seventy-two," he said. "That's gunnery sergeant Montgomery Fowler. He did three tours in Nam; won a Silver Star, a Bronze Star, and two Purple Hearts. You were sayin'?"

I stared at him. I didn't know what to say.

"T.J.," I said, shaking my head. "The big black guy can barely walk."

"Staff Sergeant Charles Wilson Massey, Chuck to his friends—of which I'm proud to say I'm one—is seventy-one. He also did three tours. He was a sniper credited with sixty-two kills, confirmed, but it was more like ninety. He took one to the shin; has a prosthetic leg. They don't come any better than him either. Oh, he also has a Bronze Star and two Purple Hearts. These men are soldiers, Harry, real soldiers, and they want to help. Let 'em."

"T.J.," I said, "you can't just pull people off the streets and—"

"Why not, Harry?" he said, with a sly smile. "You did when you took me in."

My jaw dropped. He had me there.

"Don't look a gift horse in the mouth, Harry. These two guys—they're about at the end of their time. They need something to live for. Look, I told them you were good for a couple of hundred each, but I know you better than that. You'll see them right, I know you will. Give 'em a chance. You won't regret it."

Geez, I thought, shaking my head. *If they're anything like you, I'll regret it for the rest of my days.*

I nodded, sighed, and said, "Okay." I paused, then said, "Why are *you* doing this, T.J.?"

"I owe you, man. You took me in when I was down and out. This is payback, well some anyway. Nothing I can do for you would be enough. Now, cut the crap and let's go tell 'em."

It wasn't that I'd forgotten what they looked like, but when we rejoined them in the kitchen, I took a second, long look at them. They looked like they'd just crawled out of a landfill, and they were both seated at the table eating what was left of an apple pie they'd obviously found in the fridge.

"You got coffee, boss?" the big guy, Chuck, asked.

"In the machine," I said. "Help yourselves."

"Can't. Don't know how to work it."

That, I could understand. It was a new model with all the bells and whistles—cappuccino, foam, you name it—and it had taken some figuring out, even for me. I made them a mug each.

"You guys have any idea what you're getting yourselves into?" I asked.

They looked at each other, then at T.J., then smiled up at me and nodded.

"We're goin' to war, right?" Chuck asked.

I closed my eyes, and said, "What did you tell them, T.J.?"

"Pretty much everything, I guess. Had to, didn't I?"

I sighed, resignedly, and said, "Grab your cups. I'll introduce you to the team. Oh, and you'll need some clothes."

"Already got 'em," Monty said. "T.J. took us by Walmart. We got shirts, camo pants, and jackets. We just need to change, is all."

"Great. Okay, you can wash up in here—there are towels in the drawer, there, and then you can change in the living room. Show them where and then bring them on down when they're done, T.J. I'll go warn the others."

And that's exactly what I did; the three old soldiers joined us a few minutes later. Cleaned up, though, and with a change of clothes, they didn't look too bad. I introduced them to the rest of the team.

"Oh shit," Bob said. "This is all we need. Harry."

"It's okay," I said. "These guys can carry their weight." *Sheesh,* I thought. *I sure as hell hope they can.*

"This is not happening," Kate's face was livid. "Harry, this is crazy. We don't know who they are, anything about them."

"That sounds familiar to me, Kate," T.J. said. "I seem to recall you saying something similar when you picked me up out of the gutter. I can vouch for these two. I've known them for almost fifty years. That good enough for you?"

She didn't answer him. She just nodded.

"Hello, Chuck, Monty. I'm Jacque, Harry's partner. This is Bob Ryan, and the kid is Tim. Welcome aboard. I, for one, am glad you're here." She looked at the rest of us, defiantly.

"Now, Harry," she continued. "Can we get on with

it? Will you please tell us what the plan is?"

And that was basically all there was to it. Fifteen minutes later, the two men had been integrated into the team and were acting like they belonged there.

The plan? Well, I did have one, sort of. It wasn't much, but I figured it was better than nothing.

Rose and the baby were already in the air heading for Puerto Rico, so that was taken care of. August would be going wherever I went so I could keep him safe. Amanda was under guard at the hospital. I would have liked to go see her, *maybe for the last time,* I remember thinking, but that was out of the question; the clock was ticking. We had to get out of the city, and fast.

My plan was to go to my cabin in the Northwest Georgia mountains—actually, it's more than just a cabin, but I'll get to that later. It's located northwest of New Hope in the Cohutta Wilderness area, on a bald knob just about as far away from civilization as I could get. That was by design, though it turned into something of a white elephant. My idea when I bought the place had been to use it as a getaway... Yeah, it was one of those wilderness homes and the getaways? In the six years I'd owned the place, I'd been up there only three times. *What a waste of $350K.*

One thing I'd made sure of, though, the place was self-sufficient. It had its own rainwater tank, solar panels, and a damn great gas-driven generator. Over the years, I'd made sure the place was kept in good repair. I had a couple of guys I trusted go up there several times a year to maintain it and keep the area around the house clear from encroaching undergrowth.

Well, that was what I hoped, but I hadn't seen the place since the senator and I... Well, that's another story too, and one I won't go into here, and it was more than three years ago. What condition the place was currently in—what I was likely to find when we left Riverview that day—I had no idea.

So by the time the introductions were over, it was already pushing two o'clock in the afternoon. I wanted out of there, but there was still too much to do.

"We'll take Bob's Hummer. That okay, Bob?"

He nodded.

"Thanks—" I was going to continue, but T.J. interrupted me.

"I'll take the boys in my pickup," he said.

The old, blue 1968 Chevy C-10 was a classic with a 327 V-8 backed by a four-speed manual transmission. It had cost him a bundle, and he was still paying for it. It was the ideal vehicle to navigate the tracks and trails where we were headed, but I wondered why he was so keen to risk his baby. I didn't learn that until later, but I'm getting ahead of myself.

"Well," I said, "if you're sure."

"I'm sure," he looked at his buddies and grinned; they grinned back at him.

I have a feeling, I thought, *that I'm going to regret this too.*

"Okay, so that's the transpor—"

"I'm gonna need to take the van," Tim said.

"There's no way," I said. "It wouldn't make it up the mountain.

"Well, I got stuff in it I gotta have."

"What stuff?" I asked.

"Stuff—you know—stuff."

I didn't know, and I didn't want to.

"There's no room for a bunch of electronics and gizmos," I said. "You can take your laptop. That's all you need, right? And don't forget to put that GPS tracker back where you found it."

"*Nooo,*" he all but howled. "We need the drone, and I have a bunch of cameras I need to bring. There might be something else. I don't know. I need to think about it some more."

"Get it together, Tim," I said, quietly. "And do it quickly. I don't have time for your nonsense."

He snorted once, rose from his seat, and started rooting through the pile of—I'm going to call it crap—he'd hauled into the basement less than two days ago, muttering loudly to himself.

"I said quietly, Tim."

He turned and glared at me. I almost smiled, but I didn't. The boy needed some discipline.

I turned to Bob and said, "We need to arm those two and ourselves. What do we have left in the gun room? How much C-4 is there?"

Now you may be wondering what I was doing with C-4. It's easy enough. I'd seized it from Lester Tree back in the day when he murdered my brother Henry. Well, he didn't do it himself, one of his henchmen did that. Anyway, I just never did turn it in. Now it was going to come in useful; it already had. *Tree,* I thought, *I'd forgotten about him.*

"I dunno, eight or ten pounds, maybe," Bob said.

"Other than that, there's not a whole lot left: a couple a 12-gauge, an old Savage 30-06 bolt action rifle, and a couple of antique 1911 semi-autos. That's about it."

Crap, I thought. *Is that it? Add that to the four M400s and our puny handguns, and we were not only outnumbered, but we were also totally outgunned to boot.*

"Geez," I said, looking at the three amigos. "It's not much, but it will have to do."

They said not a word, just sat there smiling, like three all-knowing godlets.

"Nothing to say?" I asked.

"I have what I need," Chuck said, looking up at me, still smiling.

"Me too," Monty said, also still smiling.

I looked at T.J. He shrugged and gifted me with one of those huge tight-lipped smiles.

Oh yeah, I'm going to regret it.

"Okay," I said to Bob, "go get everything you can lay your hands on: the C-4, detonators, ammo, everything. Take Kate with you. As soon as you get back, we'll leave. It's a good ninety-minute drive to the cabin, so I want to be away from here no later than 4pm... Oh, wait. You'd better grab my Spider. I hate that thing, but it saved my life last time I wore it." *Yeah, it sure as hell did. I took six from Calaway and lived to tell about it.*

I turned to Tim. He was still muttering quietly to himself, but the stack of what he wanted to take with him had been reduced to the drone case, two more aluminum cases, and a top-of-the-line Macbook. It was more than I wanted, but I had a feeling he wasn't about to give up any more of his toys.

18

SATURDAY, MAY 26, 5:25PM

Cohutta Wilderness
I'd thought at first that my ninety-minute estimate was a bit ambitious, but fortunately, we'd had a dry spell. The forest roads and tracks were hard, though rough going, and we made it to the cabin with five minutes to spare.

"Oh, my God, Harry," Jacque said. "It's beautiful but so remote."

"Hah," Kate said, dryly. "That it is. A girl could scream her head off and no one would hear her."

She was right; they both were. The next nearest dwelling was at least a half-mile away. The cabin—that's not really a good description—was built in the early sixties by a reclusive millionaire. He died there. His body wasn't discovered for more than a month.

The place is a huge, elevated two-story log house built from pine logs twenty inches in diameter; big enough to stop a bullet. It was surrounded on all sides by an eight-foot-wide porch and sat on a poured, reinforced concrete basement. It even had a hot tub, as T.J., to his delight, quickly discovered. How the hell the original owner had gotten the materials up there to build it, I never asked. There are, however, companies that specialize in the construction of this type of wilderness home.

The first thing I did, when we arrived up there at just before five-thirty that afternoon, was check the inside of the house. What a frickin' mess. Unfinished meals on the kitchen table, sideboard, and sink drainer. Trash covered just about every inch of the floor; beds had been slept in and in disarray. There was no one present in the house, but it was obvious someone had been living there, and maybe still was.

I was even more astonished to find the pantry was well-stocked: no perishables, but enough canned foods and dehydrated survival meals, a lot of survival meals, to feed an army. I checked the freezer; it was crammed full of frozen meals. *What the hell's been going on?*

I had no idea, but I soon found there was more to come. By the time I gave it up inside the house and went back outside, Bob had parked the Hummer out of sight, around the back on the south side of the house over-looking the gorge. T.J. had parked his truck on the same side but under the porch, well out of sight, and close to the steel, basement door.

"Hey," I said to Bob in a low voice. "Someone's living in the house. There's trash everywhere."

"But there's no one here now, right?"

"I didn't see anyone," I said so only Bob could hear. Then I raised my voice and addressed the whole group.

"Okay, listen up, people. Get the gear out of the vehicles and into the house, through here."

I unlocked the basement door and opened it. The interior was dark, smelled musty, damp even, and... gasoline? I turned on the lights, stepped inside, and got the shock of my life. The west wall was lined with weapons of all shapes and sizes, enough to start a small war.

"Geez," Bob said, looking over my shoulder. "Where the hell did you get this stuff?"

"I didn't. It's not mine. It must belong to the Thackers, Ricky and Bubba. They're a couple of good-old-boys I've known for years, trusted them. I pay them to maintain the place. What the hell is all this, I wonder?"

"Looks like a gift from the gods, if you ask me," T.J. said, muscling his way through the door. "Wow, look at that, Chuck, a Barrett M107 .50 caliber rifle."

"Two of them," he said, enthusiastically, "and scopes. Geez, I wish I'd had one of them back in Nam. Makes my Ruger look like a peashooter."

I looked at the stash. I couldn't believe what I was seeing. On the west wall were three racks that between them held a collection of at least a hundred assorted firearms, ranging from the Barretts to an antique Remington to several Henry repeaters, AR15s; there was even an AK-47. Stacked against the north wall, under the stairs, were dozens of steel ammo cases. In the southeast corner were six one-hundred-gallon drums; one had a hand pump. *I guess that accounts for the smell of gas,* I thought.

"Just how well do you know these two 'good old boys'?" Bob asked.

"I met them years ago; handy-men. I had them do several small jobs for me. Seemed like a good idea to have them look after the house. I've met them maybe three times since."

"Looking at this stash, I'd say that maybe these guys are white supremacists, and they're squatting in your house, Harry," Bob said.

"Harry," Kate said, urgently. "Listen. Someone's coming."

I swung around, listened; she was right. I could hear an engine grinding away in the distance.

19

SATURDAY, MAY 25TH, 5:45PM

The Thackers

I pulled my gun, so did Bob, Kate, Chuck, and T.J. while Monty ran to the back of T.J.'s truck, opened the toolbox, and withdrew a 1960-era M16.

"*August, Tim, Jacque,* get inside the basement, now. Close the door and stay there. The rest of you spread out, but don't do anything unless I give the word. I don't want anybody killed... Not yet, anyway."

And we waited, silently: T.J. and Monty out of sight beyond the tree line; Kate, Bob, and Chuck were spread out around the house. Me? I sat at the bottom of the porch steps, looking down the trail, listening as the straining engine grew louder... And then it appeared, a battered old Ford F250 FWD jerking and rocking as it slowly dragged itself up the rutted trail.

I could see that there were three men in the front seat. I stood, took several steps forward, and leveled my VP9 at the driver.

"Stop!" I shouted. "Get out of the vehicle and down on the ground. *Do it. Now.*"

Both doors flew open. "Don't shoot, Mr. Starke. It's just me an' Bubba an' Otis."

Geez, it's the frickin' Thacker brothers.

The three men scrambled out of the cab and dropped flat on the ground, their legs and arms spread-eagled. *Hah, they've done that before.*

"Don't move," I said, walking toward them. "Stay right where you are. Bob, Kate, pat them down."

All three of them were carrying. Between them, they had two Colt Pythons, three .45 1911s of varying brands, and—I couldn't believe it—a .50 caliber Desert Eagle, one of the most powerful handguns on the planet.

"Sit up," I said.

Ricky and Bubba, I already knew. Otis, a small, skinny individual with lank, dirty blond hair, I didn't know—he was the one carrying the Eagle. *Geez, if he ever fired that thing, it would lift him off his feet.*

The Thacker brothers are identical twins, handsome, bearded, reminded me a little of Keanu Reeves, but where he's a very smart guy, these two were... not quite dumb, but certainly not so smart.

"Hey, you guys in the basement," I shouted. "It's okay, you can come on out."

I waited for them to join us, then said, "Okay! Talk to me, Ricky. What the hell have you been doing up here? I pay you to maintain the place, not live in it."

"An' that's zackly what we do," he said, nodding enthusiastically. "Maintain the place. We come up here maybe once a month and spend a couple days workin' around the place. It takes time, you know?"

"Bullshit, and no, I don't know. You've been living in my house. Explain."

He looked at the other two. Bubba shrugged. Otis didn't react.

"Okay, so look," Ricky said, earnestly. "You ain't been up here in more'n two years. An', well, it's quiet up here, nobody ever comes. So I, we, figured you wouldn't mind if we come an' stayed a piece, do a little huntin' an' shootin'. We ain't hurt nothin', an' we kept the place up, mostly."

I stared at him, lowered my weapon, waved at the others to indicate all was well, then said, "What about all this?" I asked, waving the VP9 at the small pile of unbelievable firepower. "And all of the weapons in the basement, and the food. How the hell long did you figure on squatting in my house?"

"It ain't like that, Mr. Starke. We were just layin' in some supplies." He paused, took a deep breath, then continued, "Okay, it's like this. See, we figure that, come the revolution, an' it surely is comin', Mr. Starke, and sooner than you might think, why..." He caught the look I was giving him and got back on point. "Well, we thought we'd, an' you too, Mr. Starke, better be prepared for the cattyclis... the cattyclis... Oh hell, what's the frickin' word?"

"Cataclysm," I said.

"Yeah, that," he said. "So we laid in a few things. See, we reckon that we can bring the girls up here an' hold for months. An', well that's it. We gotta be able to survive, right?"

I wanted to smile, but I didn't. I looked at my people. With the exception of Kate, they were all smiling.

"So what're you doin' here, Mr. Starke?" he asked, amicably. "You come for some fishin'? Huntin', maybe?"

"Fishing?" Bob asked. "Where the hell can you fish up here on top of a frickin' mountain?"

"There's a lake about a quarter-mile that way," I said.

"Get your stuff together, Ricky," I said, "and get out of here. You're fired."

"Oh, come on now, Mr. Starke. We ain't hurt nothin', an' besides, it'll take us hours to—"

"You'd best get started then. Get to it. Now."

"Oh man!" he said, "Okay, c'mon boys, do as the man says." And, grumbling among themselves, the three turned, picked up their weapons, climbed back into the truck, and drove around to the basement door.

20

SATURDAY, MAY 26, 6PM

C**ohutta Wilderness**
 I checked my watch. It was almost six. I figured we had maybe two, two-and-a-half hours of daylight remaining; we had a lot to do.

"Okay," I said, "they may not come, but I think they will. We need to prepare for the worst. There are six of us not counting August, Tim, and Jacque."

"I can—"

"No," I said, interrupting August. "You'll stay out of it. That's not up for discussion."

If looks could kill. Well, it's a good job they can't, because the look August gave me would have shriveled a Saguaro cactus. Fortunately, though, he took me at my word and said nothing.

"Now," I said, "to continue, I want firing stations at the front and both sides; the back shouldn't be a problem. The gorge is too steep—"

"Harry," Bob said, interrupting me, "you're forgetting

these guys are Rangers. It's highly likely they'll do just that, the unexpected, and use scaling equipment."

I thought for a minute. He was right. In my mind's eye, I could see them scaling the gorge wall and come storming over the top.

"You're right," I said. "Stupid of me not to think of it. So, until we know what they're up to, let's have two at the front; that would be you and me, Bob. Chuck, you and T.J. take the back. Monty, you take the east end; Kate, you take the west end." I turned my head to look at Tim.

"You still up to it, son? If not—"

"I am. You need me to fly the drone, right? And communicate, as we did last night?"

Last night? Is that all it was?

"Yes, that's what I need. Can you do it without—"

"Getting my head shot off?" he asked, Interrupting me. "Sure can. All I need to do is launch it. I can set it out on the porch ready to go and fly it from in here. I'm just about ready. I'll monitor it on my laptop. You'll need the earbuds and, if you intend to go outside, the body cams."

I looked at Jacque. "You look after August, okay?" She nodded. "Oh, for God's sake," he muttered.

And, Jacque, make sure that Glock is locked and loaded. If anyone comes in through the back door don't hesitate, shoot to kill." And I had no doubt that she would, and even less doubt that she could; I'd taught her to shoot myself.

"Okay, we'll think about the rest of those details later, when we get done outside," I said. "Right now, T.J.," I turned to him and said, "you and Monty take some of that C-4 and head north up the slope." I looked out of the window. Beyond the trees, the rocky mound that was the top of the mountain rose another thousand feet.

"If they do come," I said, thoughtfully, "I figure it will most likely be from that direction. So get yourselves up there into the trees and lay down some trip wires. There's nylon fishing line in the basement. Well," I said, thinking about the Thackers, "there'd better be. Try to cover the approaches through the trees from the north. Cover as much ground as you can. Okay, everyone, let's get to it."

I waited until they'd left, then said, "How about you, Chuck? I heard you say that you have a weapon, right?"

"I do, it's still in T.J.'s pickup, a Ruger Precision Rifle chambered for 6.5 Creedmoor. It's good, but I'd sure like to get my hands on one of them .50 cals downstairs."

"Go get you one," I said. "Tell Ricky I said so, and that he still owes for the mess." And he did.

"Kate," I said, "are you okay?"

"No, Harry, I'm not. I can't believe this is happening. Have we all gone mad?"

I smiled at her, put a hand on her arm, and said, "I know. It's crazy, but we didn't start this. We have no choice, at least I don't. But you still do."

"The hell I do. How would I leave?"

"You've got a point. I wish—"

"Eh, you know what they say about wishes. Don't worry, Harry. I'll do my bit. I just hope to hell no one gets killed."

"Me too, Kate. Me too."

~

"Hey, Mr. Starke!"

I was on the back porch overlooking the gorge. I'd returned to check on the Brothers Grimm, to see how much longer they were going to be. I wanted them out of there before the crap hit the fan.

"Yeah, what. Why are you still here?"

"It's seven-thirty. It'll be dark soon. It's too late for us to try to make it down the mountain. We could get ourselves killed. We'll stay till mornin' and—"

"You'll go now."

"No, sir. We will not. It ain't right. You cain't expect us to kill ourselves. We ain't gonna do it. What the hell are you guys doin' anyway? Looks like you're preparin' for a fight."

I pulled my VP9, but before I could point it at him, Bob laid a hand on my arm and said, "He's right, Harry. Let 'em stay."

I hadn't even heard him coming.

"I can't, Bob. If Christmas sends in his troops—"

"If he does," he said, interrupting me, "the extra fire-power will come in handy."

"Oh, you've got to be kiddin' me. Those three? They're idiots playing some sort of survival game."

"No, we ain't," Ricky shouted. "We're ready, man. Who we talkin' about, the army? Let 'em come. Otis here can shoot the eye out of a squirrel at five hundred yards. Though you'd never be able to know it, not after it bin hit by one o' them fifty cals. It don't matter though. I ain't riskin' a ride down Old Baldy at night, no matter what you say."

I shrugged, turned away, and said, "Your choice, Ricky. I hope you live long enough to regret it."

"Hey wait. Where we gonna sleep?"

"Anywhere you like, so long as it's outside."

"Oh, ma-an."

I smiled and continued on into the house.

"Harry," Bob said, following me in. "If they're staying, that means the road will need to be... Okay, listen, I have an idea, so I'm going to see what I can do about it. I'll be back in as soon as I can."

And, without waiting for an answer, he ran down the stairs into the basement. What he had in mind, I had no idea. I had plenty on my own mind, and I needed to get on with it.

By eight that evening, we were all back together in the living room, with the exception of the Thackers and Otis. The work outside had been taken care of. We'd done as much as we could in the short time that we had. All we could do now was sit and wait.

And we did, and it was one of the worst experiences you can ever imagine. The lights inside the house were mostly off, all except for a small end table lamp in the living room; the windows were open so we could hear. Outside, there was still some light left but, other than the sounds of the night—the insects and the occasional call of an owl—all was quiet. We watched, and we listened. My mind began to wander, and then I remembered something.

"Bob, do we have any C-4 left?" I asked, thoughtfully.

"Yeah, we still have four half-pound packs."

"Good. Do you see that deep rut in the trail down

there?" I pointed at it. "You hit that on our way up here, remember? So did Ricky. I saw him. There's no way to avoid it."

"Gotcha," he said grinning. "I'm on it."

"Wait," I said, placing a hand on his arm. "Is it close enough for you to wire it to a trigger?"

The grin grew wider. "Just about. I gotta go."

It took him about fifteen minutes to set the AID—two pounds of C-4 in an empty paint can buried in the center of the rut.

"Hey," he said when he returned. "I already booby-trapped the trail a ways back. I don't think anyone will make it past it, but if they do, I'm gonna be the one to trigger this thing, right?" He held it up for me to see.

I smiled, and said, "You got it, brother."

I settled down again with my back to the window... and then, some thirty minutes later, I heard it; the sound of an airplane engine, and it was approaching fast.

21

SATURDAY, MAY 26, 7:30PM

T he Battle of Cohutta Wilderness
        "Shit! That sounds like Nick's King Air
        jump plane," Bob said."

My heart sank. I'd been expecting something, but...

I checked my watch. It was eight. "You were right, Tim," I whispered, though why I was whispering... No one was in earshot... yet!

"Just like I said," Tim said, grinning.

Does nothing ever bother that boy?

"Yeah, well," I said, "it matters little. It's what we wanted. I just wasn't expecting them quite so soon, is all. It's still quite light."

But that wasn't all, I could hear a powerful diesel engine hauling up the trail."

"Okay," I said, "August, Jacque, basement, now! Everyone else, weapons check."

"Harry," August said as he rose to his feet.

"Not now, Dad. Just do as I ask, please. Go with Jacque." And he did, though reluctantly.

I racked my VP9, reholstered it, hauled back on the bolt of my M400 and let it slam back, ramming a cartridge into the chamber.

"Vests," I said as I jumped up, went over to the couch where I'd dumped my Spider tactical vest, grabbed it, checked the ceramic plates in the sleeves, chest, and back and then climbed into it. I hadn't worn it since my fiasco with Calaway Jones. It still felt like I was wearing a straitjacket.

The sound of the engines grew louder. They were almost on us. Ready or not, we were out of time.

"How many jumpers can that thing carry, Bob?" I asked.

"Fifteen."

"Holy shit. I wonder what the hell is coming up the trail."

"Sounds big, whatever it is."

"Get ready everyone," I said, tersely. "Tim, get that thing into the air, and for God's sake keep your head down."

Tim didn't answer. He was seated on the floor with his back to the north wall, busy jiggling the controls. I watched him, shaking my head. He was like ice, concentrating, methodical, and then he began his commentary.

"We're at five hundred feet and climbing, six hundred, seven... one thousand. I see nothing... Wait, there's something moving on the trail. It looks like... It's a freaking Humvee..."

He was interrupted by the clatter of an automatic rifle somewhere back down the trail.

"Well, there goes that surprise," Bob said, with a sigh.

"I figured it would tear up the cab of a pickup, and anyone inside it, but a Humvee? I doubt they even felt it. They'll feel this, though."

He held up the C-4 trigger for me to see and grinned.

The sound of the aircraft engine grew louder, so did the sound of the Humvee. I got up onto my knees and peered out of the window; I couldn't see the aircraft, but I figured it must be somewhere to the north, beyond the mountain.

"Tim," I said, "where's that pesky aircraft?"

"I can't see it... Wait, there it is. Maybe a mile away to the north, beyond the ridge. It's circling. I doubt you can see—"

BAM!

He was interrupted by the most terrific bang I'd ever heard. It had come from somewhere behind the house. *Oh shit! They* are *coming up the gorge.*

And then the door to the kitchen burst open and the three hillbillies rushed into the room, Ricky carrying an AR15, Bubba the AK47, and Otis had the second Barrett fitted with a scope the size of a beer barrel, and the Desert Eagle strapped to his right leg. Would you believe it? That rifle was bigger than he was, and the muzzle of the Eagle hung below his knee. It would have been funny if the situation hadn't been so serious.

"Weehooo," Ricky shouted at the top of his voice. "Otis done got him. He got that damn plane. You see that? Did you see *that?*"

"No, he didn't," Tim said. "I can still see it."

"No shit?" Ricky was outraged. "I know 'e did. You sure? Oh man. Sheeeit. Give 'im another one, Otis."

"Stop it, for God's sake," I shouted. "Shut the hell up, Ricky. I can't hear myself think."

"Quiet, damn it!" Bob shouted, then. "Watch now, Harry," Bob said, quietly, peering out of the window. "It's almost there..."

At that point, T.J., Chuck and Monty abandoned their firing positions at the rear and rushed into the room.

"What the hell was that?" T.J. shouted.

"It was Otis," Ricky, yelled, excitedly. "He shot the damn plane."

"*Quiet!* I need quiet, damn it," Bob shouted. "And get down."

Everybody, those that were still on their feet, dropped to their knees at the windows and we watched, and we waited, no one seemed to be breathing. Even Ricky managed to keep his mouth shut.

Slowly, the big armored vehicle lumbered out of the trees, rounded a slight bend in the trail.

"Wait for it," Bob whispered to himself. "Wait..."

The driver's side front wheel rose over a bump in the hard surface, then dipped down into the deep rut and...

Bob jerked his hand upward as he thumbed the button.

The explosion was ear-shattering, mind-rending. The vehicle rose, almost in slow motion, so it seemed, twisting in the air, then flipped over onto its side and lay still, as dead as the dinosaurs that once roamed the forests of the Cohutta Wilderness.

Yes, the vehicle was finished, but its occupants? Not so much. The doors flew open and four men dressed in full combat gear, including helmets and body armor, clambered out onto the driver's side of the stricken vehicle.

I didn't wait. I opened fire with my semi-auto M400. I saw a single puff as one of my slugs slammed into the armored shoulder of one of the men, knocking him off the Humvee. He flipped over and disappeared down between the wheels, out of sight. The other three men quickly followed him and, taking cover behind the vehicle, began to return fire with fully automatic weapons. I ducked down out of sight, so did everyone else in the room.

Within seconds, every pane of glass in all four front windows was shattered, and great shards of wood, torn from the log walls outside, spun through the air like tiny spears; bullets whined in through the windows, slamming into the walls, smashing pictures, light fixtures, wall ornaments... The noise was unbelievable: it was as if the house was being torn apart by a tornado. And then, everything went quiet.

I waited, looked around at the others. Kate had her back to the wall, her knees to her chest, head down, hands over her ears, and so it was with just about everybody else; the exception being Tim. He too had his back to the wall, but he had his ears stuffed full of buds and, the idiot was still flying his drone.

"Everybody okay?" I asked.

They all indicated that they were, with Tim being the exception.

I rose up on my knees and peered out of the window, just in time to see two men run from behind the Humvee, heading east along the tree line, toward the west end of the house. I raised my AR, but I was too late: they were both cut down by a hail of automatic fire from the window in the next room at the west end of the house.

"Oh yeah," I heard Monty yell.

What the hell?

I leaned back on my haunches, looked sideways through the open bedroom door. I could see him on his knees at the window.

"Like ridin' a freakin' bike." He was excited. "Fifty freakin' years, man, an' I still got it."

I could see that both men outside were down; one lay still, the other on his back, writhing in pain, clutching his right thigh, blood seeping from his wounds. *So much for not killing anyone,* I thought, wryly. Then, inwardly, I shrugged. *So frickin' what. It was them or us.*

As I watched, Monty raised the old M16 to his shoulder and sighted through the optic, and I realized what he was about to do.

"No, Monty. I need him alive."

"Ah shit," he said, lowering the weapon.

I turned my attention back to the Humvee, just in time to see a third heavily armored man make a break for the trees.

Then, the world ended, or so I thought. There was an enormous explosion just to my right, and the running man was lifted at least two feet off the ground before he slammed face first onto the rocky floor.

The concussion from the blast almost knocked me over; it pounded the walls, ceiling, floor, and my eardrums, and everyone else's, including Otis', who was slammed backward and down onto the floor by the recoil of the big rifle. Had he been just a little less skinny, and had he been properly set up, he could probably have handled it. As it was, he banged the back of his head hard on the wooden floor.

"You crazy piece of shit," Kate yelled. She'd dropped her AR and had both hands to her right ear. "Ow! Oh, my God. He was three feet from my head. He's busted my eardrum. Damn."

I stood, walked to where Otis still lay on his back, groggily shaking his head, and I grabbed him by the front of his camo jacket and hauled him to his feet.

"You *ever* fire that thing inside the house again, and I'll stuff it up your ass and blow you inside out. You got that?"

He nodded, weakly, squirmed. "Yeah, yeah, I got it," he said gasping. "Not in the house."

I sure as hell hoped so. My ears were ringing. God only knew what Kate and the rest of the crew were going through. Gunfire, any caliber, in an enclosed area, like the one we were in, is bad enough, but a .50 cal... Why the hell do you think we wear ear protectors, even at an outdoor range? Geez, I have to laugh when I see the likes of Tom Cruise or Keanu Reeves banging away and not the slightest flinch. In the real world, it just isn't that way.

I changed the mag on my AR, looked out of the window. All was quiet. Two men down and still, one wounded, and another... somewhere behind the Humvee, I supposed.

"Where's the plane, Tim?" I asked.

No answer. He continued working the drone controls.

I flipped one of the buds out of his ear and asked again.

"Gone. It circled away to the north and disappeared behind the top of the mountain."

"Any jumpers?" T.J. asked.

"Not that I saw, but I can't hear it, so the plane is definitely gone."

"Must have dropped 'em beyond the knob," Chuck said.

"Yeah," Bob said. "If so, we can expect 'em to be here in thirty minutes, maybe less."

I nodded. "Right. Ricky, get that crazy bastard and his cannon out of here. Find a place for him outside the house where he can do no more harm, to us anyway. Chuck," I said turning to him, "you better do the same, but go west about fifty yards. There's a rocky outcrop that should work well for you."

I stepped over to where Kate was holding her ear. "How are you doing?"

She looked up at me. "My eardrum. I think it's busted. It's bleeding, look." She held out her hand. Her palm was covered in blood. "I can't hear out of it, Harry." Her face was white.

I squeezed her shoulder. There was nothing I could say to make her feel any better, so I said nothing. I returned to my place at the window and kneeled down again, staring up through the gathering darkness at the silhouette of the crest, outlined against a clear, purple sky, and I waited, and I watched. The only sound to be heard was the wounded soldier, groaning.

"Hey, Bob," I said, getting to my feet. "Come with me. We need to get him inside, make sure he doesn't bleed to death. T.J., Tim, the rest of you, keep watch for any signs of movement out there. I don't want us to get caught out in the open. T.J., keep an eye on that Humvee. If that guy is still alive, and he shows himself, take him out."

"You got it, boss."

I nodded. "Kate, how are you feeling?

She looked up at me and shook her head, grimacing in pain.

"Well, just try to take it easy," I said. "Let's go, Bob." I opened the front door, peered outside, nothing; all was quiet.

I turned and looked at Chuck, quizzically. He nodded, raised his AR to his shoulder, and aimed it at the Humvee.

We stepped cautiously out onto the porch and then headed down the front steps. The wounded soldier was some fifty yards away to the east.

I started to run toward him. I could hear Bob following me, close up.

We dropped to the ground next to him, one on either side. I checked his wound. A round had gone clean through his upper right thigh. The exit wound was quite small, so it must not have hit the bone. The wound was bleeding, but not enough for him to bleed out. *Lucky bastard*, I thought.

"Okay, son," I said. "We're going to get you inside. Hold tight."

"Screw you," he wheezed, breathlessly.

"Yeah, of course," I said, sarcastically. "Grab his arm, Bob."

He did, and together we hauled the man back to the house, through the living room, into the kitchen and then into the laundry room, and dumped him on the floor.

"You-you-you freakin' sons o' bitches," he whispered, his face, blackened with shoe polish, twisted with pain as he fought to get the words out. "You've no frickin' idea what's about to come down on you. You're all frickin' dead; you just don't know it."

Bob reached out, undid the man's helmet strap, and hauled it off his head.

"Well, well," Bob said. "Hello, Johnny. It's been a long time. Harry, say hello to Johnny Pascal. He's one of Nick's people. I met him, just once. He was with Nick in Kandahar. How is Nick, Johnny? Is he up there somewhere?"

"Screw you," Pascal said, between teeth that were clamped shut. "I've never seen you before in my life, an' I've never been to Afghanistan. An' who the hell is Nick?"

Bob laughed. "Yeah, right," he said. "How about I leave you here to bleed to death?" And he turned to walk out the door. I started to follow.

"Wait. You can't let me die. Please?"

We turned. "So, tell us what the plan is," I said, quietly.

"I don't know. No, honestly. They don't tell me anything. I'm just a peon. Yeah, I work for Nick, but I'm just one of the troops."

Bob looked at him, then said, "Makes sense, Harry.

Nick always was a tight-lipped son of a bitch. You want me to patch him up?"

I stared at the wounded man, thinking. Not really, my mind was somewhere else—I was thinking about Amanda—but I nodded, and said, "Yeah, while it's quiet out there. No, on second thought, they could be here any minute. Let's get him down to the basement. Jacque can handle it. Strap his hands."

Jacque wasn't happy about it, but August said he'd help. She looked squeamishly at the man's blood-soaked pants, then made up her mind, steeled herself, reached into her pants pocket, took out a folding knife, opened it and set to work cutting his pants. I grinned at Bob, and we left them to it.

"See anything?" I asked the group as Bob closed the basement door.

"Nope," T.J. said.

"Tim?" I asked. No answer.

I sighed, stepped over to him and was about to yank one of his earbuds when he looked up at me.

"What?" he said, removing one of the buds.

"What's going out there?"

"I'm not sure. The plane has gone, and I'm not seeing any movement. I have the drone at five-thousand feet, and I'm sending it north, beyond the crest, to see if I can find anything. Wait... look, there." He pointed to a spot on the screen. "There they are. Those are heat signatures—one, two, three-four-five—I make twelve of them."

I knelt down beside him, squinted at the almost black screen. At first, I couldn't see anything, but then I could make out the small red dots moving slowly through the trees.

"I'm too high," he said. "I need to lose altitude. Then we'll be able to see better."

"Be careful, Tim. If they hear that thing—"

"They won't. It's almost silent... There, how's that?"

The red dots had turned into blobs, and he was right: there were twelve of them.

"How far, Tim? How long do we have?"

"It's hard to tell; too dark, but maybe..." He looked up at me. "Maybe a little more than a mile, say fifteen, twenty minutes at most."

"How much longer can you keep that thing in the air?" I asked.

He looked at a ticking timer in the corner of the screen, "Fourteen more minutes, then I need to change batteries."

"Get it back here and do it now. We need the eye. How long will it take?"

He thumbed the controls, the image on the screen tilted, blurred, then adjusted itself. Even I could tell it was moving fast.

"Get the case for me, Harry. Sorry, but I need to fly her."

Her? Geez, now it's a girl.

I opened the case. "Okay," I said. "Now what?"

"You should be able to see four sets of batteries. They're in packs of three. I need one of those, then I need you to go out onto the porch and grab the drone and bring it in here."

"You can't go outside to it?"

He looked up at me plaintively, and said, "It's not heavy."

And I got it. The boy was scared, and I didn't blame him, not one bit.

"Done," I said as I handed him the batteries, then stepped out onto the porch. Suddenly, it was there. I didn't even see it coming. With no more than a whisper, it settled gently at my feet, and the six propellers slowly wound down and stopped. I stooped and picked it up. It was huge: more than five feet in diameter. I had to turn it on its side to get it through the door. It took him maybe thirty seconds to change the battery pack.

"Okay," Tim said. "Go! Yell at me when you're clear."

I did as he asked, placed the drone gently down on the porch floor, stepped away, and shouted "Okay," and watched as the propellers began to spin. It lifted slowly, a couple of feet, and then it tilted slightly, and... like a giant dragonfly, was gone into the still darkening sky. I checked my watch. It was just after eight-thirty.

I returned to Tim's side and knelt down, "Do we have them?"

"Not yet... Where the hell are you?" he whispered to himself. "Ah, gotcha. There, see? Wait, I'll lose altitude. Okay, now. There!"

And there they were, twelve red blobs moving steadily up the north side of the knob.

"Oh hell," I said. "They'll be at the crest any minute."

"Lemme see," Bob said, and he came and stood behind me.

"We're out of time, Harry," he said. "Chuck, are you listening out there?"

He was; we all were, except Kate. She was seated with her back to the wall, her head back, her eyes closed.

"Yessir, loud and clear. They'll be on us any minute, right?"

"Right, so watch the crest. Anything moves up there, shoot to kill. Have you got the range?"

"I do. I make it nine-hundred-twenty yards, but whoever calibrated this scope didn't know what the hell he was doing, so it's a crapshoot if I hit anything, or not. I'll do my best though."

"Don't worry," Monty said, slamming a full mag into his M16. "He's jerkin' your chain. He won't miss."

I raised my own M400 and sighted through the scope at the ridgeline. It was tough to see anything in the darkness, but I adjusted the focus, and the dark line of the ridge against the now deep purple sky leapt sharply into focus. As far as I could tell, nothing was moving... and then... a tiny, black figure appeared, then another, and another.

Bam! Bam! Two shots from two Barretts, and one of the figures disappeared. I saw it happen, but... it was too quick. One second it was there, the next it was gone.

"Yay, Chucky," I heard Monty yell in my ear. "You got 'im, man."

"Like hell he did," a strange voice shouted in my ear. "That was me, damn it. I shot 'im." It was Otis somewhere outside and to the east.

"Like hell you did, you little shit," Chuck said.

"You dumbass son of a—" Otis started to reply, but I cut him off, both of them.

"Shut the hell up, both of you. This ain't a pissing match. Keep your freakin' eyes on that ridge and nail anything that moves."

Never for a second had I taken my eyes off the ridge. Not only had Chuck's victim disappeared—yes I figured it was him that had made the kill—so had the rest of them.

And then it began. Slowly at first, a single shot screamed in through the window and slammed into the wall on the far side of the room, and then another, and then all hell broke loose, and it seemed as if the room, all of the front rooms, were filled with hornets. I sat with my back to the wall under the window, my hands over my head, and I waited, praying. The noise was unbearable; I can only describe it as akin to the room being filled with the sound of shattering glass and thunder as the bullets hammered the interior log wall. Debris: glass, china, chunks of wood ripped from the walls flew in every direction.

Oh, they were good. I estimated that almost a hundred percent of the fire was entering the house through one window or another. There was nothing we could do but keep our heads down and wait.

I could hear Otis banging away outside, but what good he was doing who knew. I sincerely doubted that he was even getting their attention. Chuck? I heard nothing from him at all. I guessed he was biding his time.

Suddenly, there was a huge explosion up on the hillside, and then another. *The trip wires,* I thought.

And then it stopped. The sudden silence was... okay, I know it's cliché, but there's no other word for it, deafening.

"Tim," I said, "the C-4, did we get any of 'em?"

"Don't know. Can't tell. Don't think so!"

Damn!

I waited, we all did; no one moved. Several minutes passed... *This is frickin' crazy,* I thought. *We're waiting for them to come and get us. Gotta do something, now!*

I turned over onto my knees, slowly raised my head, inch-by-inch... and then there was a sharp crack of a suppressed weapon and a bullet slammed into the window sill. Three inches higher and I would have been dead. Well, it wasn't, and I wasn't.

I dropped back down again.

"Tim," I said. "What can you see?"

"They're coming, and fast. Harry, you gotta do something."

Do what? We were screwed, pinned down. All they had to do was keep us that way while they approached, then toss in a couple of grenades and we were done.

"Okay, people," I said, "listen up. They have us, or they will soon. Chuck, Otis, you gotta hold 'em while we get out of here. Kate, you're in bad shape, so you go join Jacque and August in the basement. Lock the door behind you. Keep them safe. Tim, can you keep that thing in the air a little longer?"

He nodded, but I could tell he was scared shitless.

"Okay, T.J., you and Monty stay here with Tim and keep him safe. Ricky, Bubba, go to Otis and set up a firing position, but do not open fire until you hear from me, understand?"

They didn't reply, they just ran out of the back door. To Otis or to escape? I didn't know, nor did I care.

"Bob, you and me, out the back and go right. We'll set up with our backs to the gorge between here and Chuck. Ready? Let's do it."

22

SATURDAY, MAY 26, 9PM

The Battle of Cohutta Wilderness
Part 2

Five minutes later, we were back outside, in position, and waiting.

"Harry, Bob, Chuck," Tim said in my ear. "Five hundred yards northwest. Seven—no, eight men—nine, coming down the slope through the trees directly toward the house."

I turned to look. It was too dark. I could see nothing.

"Otis?" Tim said. "Can you hear me?"

"I can!"

"Yeah, me too," Ricky said. "I'm here with him. What do you have?"

"Four hundred yards to the northeast, three more, and they're closing, fast. Oh shit—"

He was cut off by a stream of automatic fire from one of the windows in the house, followed immediately by a second, much slower volley of fire from an M400, Monty's M16, and T.J.'s AR.

"Hang on, guys," I yelled as I jumped up and started to run. "I'm on my way. Bob, Chuck, keep your eyes open. Do what you can."

Bam! Chuck fired the big rifle, and I swear the ground shook under my feet. I took no notice. I ran for the house, bullets screaming by and kicking up spirts of dust and shards of rock around me. And then, just as I made the turn to my right toward the back of the house, something slammed into the center of my back and I went down, head first, like a sack of potatoes. I lay still for a second, my head ringing, my back feeling as if I'd been stomped on by an elephant.

It felt like every nerve in my body was on fire. What the hell had hit me, I'd no idea, not then. It wasn't until later, much later, that we figured it must have been a 5.56 NATO round.

I stumbled to my feet, staggered toward the back of the building, turned left and threw myself to the ground, and I lay there, gasping for breath.

"Harry," Bob yelled. "Talk to me. Are you okay? For God's sake, Harry..."

"Yeah, yeah, I'm okay, damn it. Concentrate on the enemy, not me, damn it."

"Well okay, then. Just so long—"

"I said I'm okay, okay? Just give me a minute to catch my breath."

I lay there for what seemed like an hour but could only have been a few seconds, and then I was up on my feet and running for the steps up onto the rear porch. I slammed the door open, ran inside and joined T.J., Monty, and Tim behind the front wall of the house. T.J.

was on his knees, cool as ice, firing steadily into the darkness. Monty was firing quick, three-round bursts from the M16, at nothing I could see. Tim, bless him, had his back to the wall, his head down, his eyes glued to the screen, and was issuing a steady stream of fire directions to all three groups, inside the house, and out. The floor around the three of them was littered with expended brass cartridges.

"Boss," T.J. said. "You get hit?"

"Just a little, but the armor stopped it. I'm fine." *Like hell you are,* I thought.

I found a spot at one of the windows, dropped to my knees, peered out over the sill, and was rewarded by a half-dozen impacts as bullets slammed into the wood, inside the house and out. *Holy shit!*

But we were wearing them down.

Tim kept up a steady, excited report, not only of where they were, but also as they were hit, or at least stopped moving. Slowly, the fire from the hillside began to slow, until finally, it stopped. No, we hadn't got them all, far from it, but we'd done one hell of a lot of damage.

"I think they're regrouping," Tim said. "I make five down and seven on the move. They're converging. Seven of them, almost directly to the north—three hundred and fifty—now three-sixty yards out. Chuck, you should have a direct line of sight."

Bam! Bam!

"Looks, like, you got one of them, Chuck."

"No, he di'nt, damn it. I did," Otis yelled.

"*Otis,*" I yelled. "Shut the hell up."

"Well, he di'nt. It was me."

I let it go. It wasn't worth the hassle.

"So six left, then, Tim?" I asked.

"Looks like it. Harry, I have twenty-nine minutes of flight time left."

Oh shit! We lose that drone, we're done for.

I thought for a minute, then said, "Bob, I'm coming back out. Wait for me." Then to the group in the house, "I'll be back."

"Okay, Arnold," T.J. quipped.

"Okay," I said to Bob. "Tim, are you listening?"

"I am."

"We can't get these guys from here. We need to circle around back. There's a trail through the trees, that way, down the track, past the Humvee, to the west. Bob and I will circle around and then come down the hill at them. Tim, can you see us?"

"I can. Be-be careful, guys."

"Okay, will do. We don't have much time, so let's go."

We headed west at a fast run, stooped over, heads down, rifles cradled in our arms, down the trail, past the Humvee—out of the corner of my eye I saw the body of the fourth occupant of the vehicle—for about a hundred yards. The damn trail was hard to find in the dark; we had to slow down, but eventually, there it was. We turned right through the trees and up the mountain. We ran for maybe five more minutes then swung right along the ridge, then right again for about fifty yards and stopped. I'd thought I was in good shape, but that run just about did me in.

"Tim, you still got us?"

"Yeah, but not for much longer. You have about seven

minutes and then I'll have to pull the drone, or we'll lose it. Your targets are two hundred yards to your southeast. Go!"

And we did, and as we did, Tim guided us in, until, "That's it, guys. I'm pulling the drone. They're less than fifty yards dead ahead, go." Geez, that was the quickest seven minutes of my life.

And we looked sideways at each other, nodded, and we went.

Tim was right. We found them right where he said we would. Seven of them. We caught them completely by surprise. Dressed from head to toe in black, combat gear, armor, helmets, night vision, the works, they were spread out over maybe a hundred feet, in line abreast, their attention on the single light left burning in the house some three hundred and fifty yards away.

We separated, came at them from two different angles, and opened fire together, caught them in a semi-crossfire, pumping round after round into the group. I blasted through one thirty-round mag, stopped advancing, ejected it and slammed in another, dodged to my left and resumed my all-out charge. I saw wood, debris, blood, and flesh flying in all directions, and we cut them down... well, five of them.

I was still more than twenty yards from them when the first guy heard us, rolled onto his back and began to level his assault rifle. I managed to nail him in the face before he could pull the trigger. And then everything turned into a blur, a wild melee where time seemed to stand still. A second man went down under a hail of bullets from Bob's AR... and then

I completely lost track of what was happening around me. I dropped to my knees, dumped the second empty mag and replaced it, emptied the new one, flung the weapon aside, jerked my VP9 from its holster and emptied it, all seventeen rounds, quicker than you could count.

And then... it was over. I jumped to my feet and ran forward, the empty mag falling away. I rammed in a full one, on the run: I didn't need it.

Two of the men jumped up and ran like rats into the night. The remaining five? Their body armor had stopped most of the hits, but all five lay dead, blood oozing from wounds to heads, necks, arms, and legs.

I skidded to a stop on the loose surface of the forest floor, three feet from one of the bodies, the VP9 hanging loosely in my right hand. I was doubled over, head almost between my knees, my left hand on my knee, taking my weight. I was so out of breath; my head was spinning. I truly thought my lungs had burst.

I don't think they got off more than a couple of dozen shots between them. Unfortunately, Bob collected two of them, center mass, right in the chest; thank god for ceramic plates.

I breathed hard for several more seconds, then pulled myself together. "Bob," I gasped, looking sideways at him. "You okay?"

"Geez, Harry, I think my chest is busted. Yeah, I'm good, I think. You okay?"

"Yeah. If I could just get my breath..."

"You're outa shape, buddy..."

"Harry," I heard Tim yell in my ear. "What's the

heck's happening up there? We heard the shooting. Are you guys okay?"

"Yeah, Tim," I said, exhausted. "We're fine. We cleaned 'em out. Well, two got away, but I don't think they'll bother us anymore. Sheesh, I'm winded. Give us a minute to catch our breath, and we're on our way."

It wasn't until several days later that, when I got to thinking about it, I realized that without Tim and his toy, we would all have died up there that day: me, Bob, August, Kate—all of us. As it was, well, we did okay. We all survived, though Kate's hearing would never be quite the same, and Chuck had lost the tip of his right ear. And... we had a prisoner. I was feeling pretty good, pleased with myself, as we headed down the rise toward the house. *It's over,* I thought. *Thank God for that.*

But it wasn't. No sooner had we climbed the steps to the front door and entered the house when, in the distance, we heard a sound that turned my blood to water —the steady whump, whump, whump of an approaching helicopter.

23

SATURDAY, MAY 26, 9:50PM

The Battle of the Cohutta Wilderness Part 3

"Oh shit," Bob growled. "That has to be the damned Huey. Now we're in for it. Put that damned light out." Monty did, and Bob was right, we were in for it, and how.

T.J. jumped to his feet and ran out of the room, heading for the rear of the house. *Where the hell does he think he's going?* I wondered,

Not that it mattered, we were screwed, of that I was sure.

The Huey came sweeping in fast and low from the northeast, twin spotlights piercing the darkness, sweeping back and forth over the forest, like a pair of glistening scissor blades, searching... It disappeared to the west, the noise of its engine and rotors diminishing as it circled away to the north, around the knob, then eastward, the spotlights dimming until they finally disappeared, and all was quiet again. But that didn't last for long. Minutes later it came roaring back along the gorge, lifted up and over the house, bathing the building in light from the two spotlights, rose up to perhaps two thousand feet, tilted to one side, slid northward, then it hovered over the crest of the mountain, turned slowly until its left side was facing the house...

"Get down, *now!*" Bob screamed.

Never had an order been issued and obeyed so fast. I threw myself down and lay tight up against the wall under the window: bad mistake.

No sooner was I down and safe beneath the window, so I thought, than the sill above me, and the twenty-inch diameter log supporting it, exploded in a shower of pulverized wood and bullets. I said before that I'd just experienced the longest seven minutes of my life. That burst of fire from what I now know to be a Gatling gun, AKA a Dillon minigun, was, without a doubt the longest three seconds. That damn thing was capable of firing three thousand 7.62 rounds a minute. Can you imagine that? That's a hundred and fifty rounds concentrated on a single spot. Now count slowly to three, and you might get some idea of what it must have been like.

Again and again, the mini-gun hurled its deadly firestorm at the house and, for the most part, the great logs held, but we all knew it couldn't last. Suddenly, the clamor of the big gun stopped, and the spotlights played over the house. *They must be checking to see if we're still alive,* I thought. *Tough shit, assholes. We are. All of us, I think.*

I looked around to see if that were true. *Oh yeah, at least for now.*

I ventured up onto my knees and peered over the remains of the window sill... just in time to see a streak of fire lance upward into the night sky from somewhere behind the house and hurtle toward the still hovering Huey. *Oh my God; it's a freaking missile.*

It hit the Huey just forward of the tail rotor and exploded, severing it from the fuselage. The tail rotor flipped over backward in a shower of fire and flaming debris. The main body of the machine jerked sideways, tilted nose down, began to spin, slowly at first, then quicker and quicker as it lost altitude. Finally, it slammed vertically, nose first, into the rocky knob, exploded spectacularly with a noise like a thunderclap, and settled into a burning, melting heap of twisted metal and... bodies too, I supposed.

"What the hell was that?" I asked.

"Looked like an RPG to me," Bob said, as the basement door flew open and Kate, followed by August and Jacque burst into the room.

"Oh, my God," Kate yelled. "What *was* that? Are they gone?"

"Harry," August rushed to me, "Are you hurt? Is anyone hurt?" I told him I was fine, though I'm pretty sure he didn't believe me.

Jacque? Bless her, she collapsed in the middle of the floor and burst into tears.

And then the kitchen door opened and T.J. sauntered in, grinning widely. "Hey, y'all," he said. "I'm... ba-ck. Everyone okay? Boy, I sure took that sucker out, did I not?" he asked, rubbing his hands together like he was washing them. Even his eyes were laughing.

I was stunned. "You crazy old bastard," I said. "What the hell was that?"

"That, boss, was an RPG 7. Cool huh? As soon as I heard they had a Huey, I er... acquired one? I had it in the toolbox on the back of my truck."

"You acquired one?" Bob asked. "Just exactly where did you 'acquire' it?"

"You can acquire anything, if you know where to look. Good thing I did, though, right?"

"Much as I hate to admit it, yeah," I said, "a real good thing." *He's gonna get us all locked up; I know he is.*

"Somebody must have seen that," Tim said, now on his knees gazing up at the dwindling flames. "There'll be cops all over the place any minute."

"I doubt it," I said. "We're too far from civilization, but even so we have to report it. There are bodies all over the hillside." I paused, counting to myself. "I make it nine, and one still alive in the basement." I looked at Jacque. She nodded.

I continued, "There's also the chopper crew, and three more at the Humvee... and there are still two mercenaries running around loose somewhere up there." I paused, thinking, trying to get a grip of the situation.

"We got lucky," I continued. "Thanks to T.J., but they'll be back. What do you reckon, Bob? You know the guy. Will they be back? And more to the point, do you think he was in that chopper?"

"Not on your life; our Nick ain't one to get his hands dirty or put himself at risk if he doesn't need to. Will he send in new troops? If he has them, yeah, I'd say so. We just cost him a bunch of money and men. And he doesn't do anything by half measure."

"So," I looked at him and said, "what's the answer? Head of the snake?"

He nodded. "Yup, and ASAP, before he can regroup. Got to, Harry. It will never be over unless we cut it off. Let's do it."

I stared at him, then at T.J., Chuck, Monty. All three just stood there grinning back at me. *Three freakin' stooges...* I pushed the thought from my head. Without them, August would be dead. So would I and Kate and... *Oh, for Pete's sake. We still had work to do.*

"Okay," I said to Bob. "The Head of the Snake it is."

"What?" Kate asked. "What are you talking about? What's going on?"

"Nick Christmas," I said. "We have to finish it, once and for all. If we don't..." I let the inference hang, unfinished.

She nodded, and said, "I get it. When? How?"

"Oh no," I said, quietly, firmly. "Not this time. Bob and I will—"

"Don't forget me," T.J. said. "I just saved all our asses. I'm in."

I turned and glared at him; he grinned back at me. I was just about to set him straight when:

"Me too," Chuck said.

"An' me," Monty said.

"Yeah..." Ricky began.

"Not one frickin' chance in hell, Ricky," I growled. "You three are done. When we leave here, I never want to set eyes on any of you; that's *ne-ver!* You understand?"

"Aw, ma-an!" Ricky said, disgusted. "What you wanna be like that for? We done good, di'nt we? Aw, crap... C'mon, man."

"No. I've had a gutful of you and your crazy friends. Now sit the hell down and shut your face, before I shut if for you."

"Well, okay then," he said, dejectedly, and he sat down on a three-legged stool, the only piece of furniture in the room that was still in one piece.

"As I said, we have to finish it, so Bob and I..." I looked at the Three Stooges, shook my head and continued, "and you three, will visit our friend in Marietta.

"And—" Tim began.

"Nope, not this time, Tim," I said, interrupting him.

"But you'll need the drone. I can stay in the van. I promise."

Oh, hell. He's right. Without him, we'd be going in blind.

"Those heat signatures; can it find them through roofs and walls?"

"Well, ye-ah."

"Okay then, but you stay in the van."

I looked at Bob, my eyebrows raised in question. He nodded. "When?" he asked, checking his watch. "We can't do it in daylight, not in the city, and we need to get out of here, and quickly."

"We need information first," I said, nodding in the direction of the basement door.

"I need for y'all to stay here for a few minutes," I said,

to the group. "Bob and I have a little something we have to do in the basement."

Kate gave me a look that could have shredded a cat.

I shrugged it off. "Gotta be done," I said and turned and followed Bob down the stairs.

24

SATURDAY, MAY 26, 10PM

Basement, Cohutta

Johnny Pascal was seated on the floor in a corner of the basement, his wrists and ankles strapped together with cable ties. Jacque had cut away his pant leg and dressed the wound with strips of towel. The dressing was clean and neat, showing only a spot of blood the size of a quarter. He looked... uncomfortable... Hmm, that doesn't quite cover it. He *was* uncomfortable, no doubt about it, but he was over the shock of the wound and was, or at least he looked as if he was, once again all Army Ranger.

Together we lifted him and sat him on an old dining chair, one of six that were stacked against the wall. Bob cut the ties that held his ankles, then fastened them to the legs of the chair.

"So," I said, lightly, pulling up a chair so I could sit down in front of him. "It's Johnny, right?"

He stared back at me, defiantly, but didn't answer.

I nodded, thoughtfully... at least it was supposed to

look thoughtful, and said, "Gotcha. Not gonna talk, and I can understand that, but here's the thing, Johnny. I need information, and only you can provide it. Now, I'm not going to torture you."

"No," Bob said, stepping in front of me, "but I am."

It was typical good cop, bad cop stuff.

Bob gripped the man's thigh, screwed his thumb into the wound, and said, "Where, exactly is—"

Pascal howled in pain, cutting him off. I grabbed Bob's hand and pulled it away.

"Bob!" I said, sharply. "That's enough!"

He turned away and grinned down at me.

"So, now look, John," I said, amiably.

"*Screw you!*" he yelled at the top of his voice, cutting me off. "You think I don't know what you two are doing? You're like a couple o' stupid kids playin' a man's game. Go to hell. I ain't tellin' you nothing."

"A man's game?" Bob asked, derisively. "You and your team, you're nothing, Johnny. We wiped out your entire force of what, sixteen so-called Army Rangers, a Humvee and a freakin' chopper, and all without losing a man. Just Harry, me, three decrepit old men, all of 'em on social security, four kids, and a woman police officer. Are you kidding me? Army Rangers, my ass. Pussy Patrol is what you are, or should I say were?"

"Like I said, screw you."

Bob looked at me askance.

I hesitated, just for a moment, then nodded and said, "Go ahead."

Bob turned and smiled at the man; it was a look of

pure evil, something I'd seen only once before when I asked him if he'd killed Congressman Harper.

He turned and walked over to the workbench, prowled from one end to the other, picking up a tool here and there and then laying it down again, until he found one he liked.

He hefted it, looked at me, then at Pascal and smiled again. Pascal? He still had the same "screw you" look on his face, but that was about to change.

"Let me sit down, Harry," Bob said. I let him.

"Now then, Johnny," he said, leaning forward so that his face was close to Pascal's. "Here's how it's going to be."

He reached out with his free hand, grasped the ragged edge of the man's cut-off pant leg and, with a quick jerk, tore the front of his pants apart exposing a pair of dirty undershorts.

"Eww," Bob said. "That's disgusting. Don't you ever change your underwear?"

"Piss off," Pascal said, but he had to squeeze the words out; he was terrified.

"No," Bob said. "Last chance, Johnny." He waved the carpet knife in front of his face. "Where's Nick, and how many men does he have with him?"

"I'm tellin' ya, I don't know."

Pascal stared at the knife, mesmerized, and his whole demeanor changed, "Look, I dunno. I don't. I swear I don't."

Bob twisted in his seat, looked up at me, smiling, and said, "What do you think, Harry?"

"I don't believe him."

He turned again to face his prey. The man's face was the color of two-day-old oatmeal. Bob shook his head slowly, looked down at Pascal's crotch, and said, "I don't know if I want to touch that dirty thing, Harry."

He looked up into Pascal's eyes, and said, "Come on, Johnny. Don't make me get my hands dirty."

"I told ya, I don't know anything. They don't tell me shit. Please don't. *No!*" he yelled as Bob grabbed his shorts and ripped them away.

"My, my," Bob said. "Who's a big boy then?"

He leaned in closer. "Eww, smelly. Geez, you're frickin' filthy, disgusting."

He lifted Pascal's genitals, gently, using the point of the blade. Pascal flinched and reared back, almost tipping the chair onto its back.

"*I told ya,*" he yelled. "*I don't know shit. Aghhhh!*"

I winced as I saw the thin trickle of blood run down between Pascal's legs, onto the seat, and drip onto the floor.

"Oh, come *on,*" Bob said, mocking him. "That was just a little nick, no pun intended. It couldn't have hurt *that* much. The next one, though, now that will hurt." He paused as if he'd had a sudden thought. Then said, "Are you married, Johnny? Girlfriend? I bet you like the ladies, right?"

Pascal didn't answer, he was shaking uncontrollably.

"Cat got your tongue? Maybe I can get that next, your tongue, that is. After I take ol' Petey here." He jiggled the knife, more blood ran down onto the floor, and then...

"Aw shit. Now look what you've done," he said, disgusted.

Shit was right, but I didn't need to look, I could smell it. Pascal was terrified; he'd lost control of both his bowels and bladder.

"Okay, Pascal. That's it. You're one filthy son of a bitch, and I've had enough. You're gonna tell me what I need to know, or I'm going to relieve you of your family jewels. Now, what's it to be?"

Pascal looked up at me, his eyes pleading. "I don't... I... I..." he tried to speak, but he couldn't get the words out. He lowered his chin to his chest and began to sob.

"Freakin' Ranger, my ass. Pussy. Okay then—" Bob said.

"Stop," I said, interrupting him.

"Get up, Bob. Let me."

"Shit, Harry. You don't have the balls for it. Although, maybe you do. You did cut that guy's little finger off last week. Have at it, my friend. You want this?" He offered me the carpet knife.

I shook my head. "No. I think he's ready to talk. If not, well, you can sit down again."

I faced Pascal and said, "How about we start over Johnny, a new leaf, so to speak, yes?"

"Yeah, okay," he whispered, but he didn't look at me.

"Where," I said, "is Nick Christmas, and how many men does he have with him? And it had better be the truth."

He was silent for a long time. I let him be, gave him time.

Finally, he looked up at me and said, "He has a barracks and offices in Marietta."

"You mean the warehouse, right?" I asked.

He nodded. "Yeah, but it's more than that. He keeps his men there, equipment: vehicles, weapons. He has an apartment on the upper floor; likes to keep an eye on the troops—his exact words. That's where he is, unless..."

"Unless what?" Bob asked.

"He goes out sometimes, to eat dinner, have a drink with Hank and Jess, but he never stays out late. He likes to—"

"Yeah," I said, "keep an eye on the troops. Jess?" I asked. "Who the hell is he?"

"Not he, she. Sergeant Roark, Jessica. They sometimes... you know."

"You know her?" I asked Bob.

"Yeah, she's a tough, good-looking broad, a ball buster. Yeah, I can see Nick and her—"

"Never mind," I said, interrupting him and turning again to Pascal.

"How many men?"

"That, I don't know, not for sure. Not so many now that this happened. He sent sixteen here, plus the chopper crew. Most of the rest are deployed. Sixteen, maybe twenty."

"Geez," I muttered to myself. That wasn't what I wanted to hear.

I looked at Bob.

He shrugged, then said, "It's gotta be done, Harry."

I nodded and turned again to Pascal.

"Tell me about the warehouse, Johnny."

"It's located on—"

"I know all that," I said, interrupting him. "Tell me about the building, the interior, the layout—and don't leave anything out."

"Shit, I dunno. Okay, okay, gimme a minute to think... It's two stories front and back. The center from north to south is one story, thirty-five... forty feet at the ridge. The upper story on the back side is all weapons storage, includin' guns, ammo, explosives. There are barrack rooms, sleeping quarters, on the ground floor along the entire east side. The ground floor front is all offices. The upper floor is the captain's living quarters. The center section is where he keeps the vehicles. There's also a firing range in the basement and more storage. There're security cameras everywhere. That's all I know, honest."

He stopped talking, looked pathetic. Bob was right. Ranger he might once have been, but he'd grown old—I figured him to be at least forty-six—and soft. In another time and place, I might even have felt sorry, but the man had just tried to kill us all. Now, he was probably quite wealthy with a lot to lose. I wondered if it was an infectious disease. I sure as hell hoped it was, and that the rest of Christmas' crew was as badly infected as Pascal. But somehow, I knew that was a forlorn hope.

"Tell me about his men. Are they all ex-military... Rangers?"

"Some, but he's hired a lot o' recruits lately. They're good, or he wouldn't have hired 'em, but they ain't like us—"

"Hah," Bob laughed, interrupting him.

"Screw you." He would have continued, but seeing the look on Bob's face, thought better of it."

"We need to see a satellite view," Bob said.

"No, this time we'll use Google," I said. "You can drive the damn streets with that. We'll get a good look at the outside of the building without ever being there. Bob, I don't suppose you thought to bring suppressors?"

"Sure did. They're in the Hummer, ammo too."

He was talking about low-velocity rounds, subsonic. Without those, suppressors—most people like to call them silencers—firearms aren't silent at all. The high velocity round, as it leaves the barrel of the gun, breaks the sound barrier and creates a sonic boom, which is what you hear, what Kate heard when that damned Barrett burst her eardrum. Anyway, if you want to silence a weapon, you need subsonic ammunition—no sonic boom, just the explosion, which is suppressed. Fortunately, Bob had brought it.

"We need to get out of here," I said, checking my watch. "It's late, real late, and we have a long way to go. Let's go bring everyone up to speed."

"What about him?" Bob asked, nodding in Pascal's direction. "We can't leave him here. If he bleeds out—"

"We can. We have to. He won't."

I spent the next ten minutes explaining to the group exactly what I had in mind.

My plan, such as it was, was first to get August, Kate, and Jacque out of danger, then go back to Riverview where we—that's me, Bob, T.J., Monty, Chuck and, of course, Tim could grab a few hours rest before we headed to Marietta. Before that could happen, though, we needed to familiarize ourselves with the layout of the warehouse, and for that, we need Tim's array of monitors.

So, with all of that explained so that everyone understood, I made sure the three revolutionaries, the Thackers and Otis, were well on their way out. Then I turned to what was left of my exhausted little army.

"Jacque, you take August and go find a motel somewhere—I don't want to know where—and stay there until this is done. You go with them, Kate. I'm not risking you getting hurt any more than you already are. Stop in at a Walmart and buy burner phones and keep them close in case you need them. Do NOT call me. Tomorrow is Sunday. We're going in tomorrow evening. So wait until Monday morning and then go home. We'll be waiting for you." *And Lordy do I ever hope to hell we are.*

Kate didn't argue, and I wasn't too surprised. She'd seen and done enough. Now I had to make sure all of this didn't blow up in her face. If it got out that she was involved in any of it, she'd lose her job and probably her freedom too.

25

SUNDAY, MAY 27

Riverview
It was after two-thirty in the morning when we arrived back at Riverview. I didn't know if Tim had been right or not when he'd said that somebody must have seen the helicopter crash. My first instinct was that I'd have to call it in soon—the house and ten acres of forest were registered to me—but that would be an admission that I'd been up there and involved, would lead to a whole lot of questions I didn't want to have to answer. Not that I was too worried: no law enforcement agency in the land could take one look at the carnage up there and deny that we acted in self-defense, but I had to protect August, Kate, and the rest of my team. My one hope was that the Thackers and Otis had got clean away. I didn't trust any one of them not to throw us under the bus.

Then there was Pascal to consider. I couldn't leave him up there bleeding... not for too long anyway, I figured an anonymous call to the local sheriff from a burner phone would solve that problem... I decided to give myself until midday and then make the call, which is what I did. I made the call and in just a couple of cryptic sentences informed the desk sergeant that I'd seen a helicopter go down, gave him the rough coordinates, then tossed the phone. As it turned out, I was worried about a problem that never arose.

We grabbed a few hours' sleep and then, after we'd downed several dozen eggs, two full pounds of bacon, two entire loaves of bread, and what had to have been a couple of gallons of coffee, we gathered around Tim's bank of monitors in the basement.

I would have liked to have gone to see Amanda, but that was out of the question, considering the situation I, that is we, were in. She would have to wait.

Just a couple of minutes after we'd finished breakfast, we, the six of us, were looking at two huge aerial views of Marietta—one wide, one close up—and two views of the surrounding streets, at street level; none of it in real time. We would have to wait another hour before that could happen. It turned out that we didn't have to.

Pascal had told the truth. There were at least a dozen security cameras, that we could see, and probably more inside. It wasn't going to be easy, that was for sure.

"Tim," I said, thinking out loud, "you remember when you hacked the camera system at Hartsfield-Jackson Airport in Atlanta?"

"Yeah, I do," he said, quickly. "I don't know about these, though, unless they belong to a government agency. Which is entirely possible, I suppose, seeing as—"

"Tim, please," I said interrupting him in full flow. "Just do it, or not."

He tapped at the keys for what seemed like an interminably long time, then whispered to himself, loud enough for all to hear, "Got it, yay!" And suddenly, instead of looking at the building from the street, we were looking out from it, at the street, from an angle high up near the roof. Tim swung around on his seat with a look of excitement on his face.

"DOD," he said, triumphantly, "Department of Defense." "Took some figuring out. I had to hack nine different agencies before I found the right one. I started with the FBI, then—okay, okay—watch this."

He tapped for several seconds more, and the image on the top right screen split into six different, smaller images, each providing a different view of the streets around the warehouse. I was dumbfounded. I had always said that Tim was the most valuable member of my staff and boy was he ever proving it that day.

"Want to see inside?"

He didn't wait for an answer. He tapped some more, and the views changed from exterior to interior, which was great, but not encouraging. There were, and I know because I counted them, sixteen vehicles parked down the center of the interior of the building, including four Humvees, two military trucks, the designations of which I didn't know—one even had a small helicopter on a trailer attached to it—and an assortment of smaller vehicles including three black Chevy Suburbans.

But what really got my attention was the number of

people. I counted thirteen, but there could have been more, a lot more.

"Can you zoom in, Tim?" I asked.

"No, sir. They're all static, well not exactly static, but I can see only what the cameras are seeing. I have no control over them, sorry."

"How many cameras are there inside the building?"

"Twelve, on this system, but there could be more. If they've installed a system of their own, well, you won't know until—"

"Until they chop us down," Bob said.

I turned and looked at him. "How much of that C-4 do we have left?"

"Very little. Three half-pound packs. Why?"

"I'm hoping we won't have to use it, but I'm thinking doors. Three should be plenty. If we cut 'em up into four-ounce packs, that will give us six. How about detonators?"

"We have plenty."

I nodded. "Can I leave that to you, then?"

"You can."

"Tim," I turned back to him. "The drone, it can pick up heat signatures inside the building, right?"

"It can, but it can't differentiate between our people and his. Out in the open, up there in the forest, that didn't matter, but inside that warehouse, it's going to be tough. Still, it's better than going in blind, right?"

"I guess," I said, wryly.

"I can hover it over the building, say at five hundred feet. From that height, I'll be able to tell you how many live bodies are within, and where they are. Once you mingle with them, though, we're screwed."

"Okay," I said. "Give me a minute, please, everyone. I need to think." I stared at the interior images, had Tim flip back and forth between cameras. I was trying to get a feel for the layout.

"Okay, Tim," I said, finally. "We know that the offices are here, on the ground floor, and we know that Christmas's quarters are directly above them, or thereabouts. See, this balcony here?" I pointed to a spot on the screen. It was really nothing more than a steel walkway protected by an iron handrail. "I'm guessing that's where he's living. There are iron stairs that provide access here. Once inside the building, those stairs will be my objective. We won't know exactly where he is until you can provide us with pinpoint locations, so we won't worry about that now."

I paused, stared at the images, then said, "The real problem will be the people living here." Again, I pointed at the screen. "I count fourteen doors, so fourteen rooms. If they have allocated more than two to a room, and I'm betting it's probably four or more, we're talking a lot of potential firepower." I rubbed my hand on my chin, considering if I really wanted to say what I was thinking. I did.

"So," I continued, "T.J., Chuck, Monty; as soon as we gain access, you go for the barracks and, one way or another, you eliminate that threat."

I caught the looks on their faces; even T.J. looked serious.

"Eliminate the threat?" Bob asked. "Are you kidding? We don't even know how many there are."

"True," I agreed, "but we do have some idea. I counted thirteen, so we know there will be at least that many, but we also know that the bulk of his people are deployed elsewhere. Pascal topped the number at twenty, and these images would seem to confirm that. I'm thinking, at worst, we're looking at twenty-four, including Christmas and his girlfriend. Any comments?"

"Yeah," T.J. growled. "We're gonna go in there and kill twenty-four professional soldiers? Have you gone out of your freakin' mind, Harry? That's frickin' murder. And anyway, it can't be done," he said, shaking his head.

I didn't have a problem with that. In fact, I'd already persuaded myself the same thing. It couldn't be done, unless...

"You're right, T.J.," I said. "But they are not who we're after. All I want is Christmas."

"Then find a way to take him outside of his fortress," Bob said. "We know he goes out, occasionally. We wait, watch, and we grab him, bring him back here and bury him on a construction site."

"Occasionally," I said. "That's the operative word. We could wait for a week before he goes anywhere. And grabbing him in downtown Marietta? No! What I'm suggesting is a surgical strike. We hurt no one unless we have to. Okay people, look," I said. "It's not my intention that we go to war, but we do need to be prepared for the worst, and the unexpected. The target is Nick Christmas. No one else."

I got up and started pacing. "We go in quietly.

Weapons suppressed, in the early hours of the morning, when everyone's asleep—"

"You hope," Bob muttered.

"Yeah, I hope. If not, well..." I shook my head, annoyed at the interruption, and continued. "T.J., you, Chuck and Monty will take up positions down the center, here, here, and here, and cover the barrack rooms. Bob and I will head straight for the stairs, here, and go after Christmas. With any luck, we can be in and out without even waking anyone else. If we do wake anyone, you guys will subdue everyone who sticks their nose out, without killing anyone unless you have to. We'll be going in late at night, so they won't be prepared. Even so, the chances are that we could have a fight on our hands. If we're lucky, we won't have to shoot anyone." *Sheesh, Harry, you should be so lucky!*

"So let me get this straight," Bob said, his voice dripping with sarcasm. "You think we're just going to walk in there and drag him out?" He shook his head in open disbelief.

"That's what I'd like to think," I replied. "Do you have a better idea? If so, let's hear it."

"Yeah, I do, I like the idea of waiting until he leaves the property and catching him out in the open, but you're right; that could take a month."

"If we do have to shoot..." I continued. "Well, you know the rules: center mass only. No fancy head, arm or leg shots. Even if you get lucky and make the hit, these are elite professional soldiers, so they'll probably still be able to shoot back. If you have to shoot, shoot to kill."

I looked at each of them in turn. No one looked

happy, and I didn't blame them. Tim? I could see he was scared witless.

"It's okay, Tim," I said. "It will—we'll be fine."

I thought for a minute more, then said, "Look, guys, you don't have to do this, really. I don't expect anyone, including you, Tim, Bob, all of you to—"

"Oh, shut the hell up, Harry," Bob said, "and get on with it."

"If you're sure..."

"We're sure," Tim said. "Carry on, Harry."

I nodded and turned my attention away from the interior views and concentrated on the exterior views provided by Google. I had Tim drive the streets around the building, stopping here and there to view the entrances; there were six of them, including huge over-head doors at the north and south ends, both had small doors beside them. The entrance to the offices and, which I assumed also provided access to Christmas' living quarters, was on the west side. There were two more entrances on the east side.

"There," I said, pointing to the big door at the south end. "That end of the building is enclosed by a steel security compound. And see these dumpsters?" There were four of them, two on either side of the enclosure. "They'll provide cover from prying eyes in the street. We can park in this strip mall lot here. It's directly opposite, and you can operate the drone from there, right, Tim?"

He nodded, thoughtfully.

"We'll travel in two vehicles: Tim's van and Bob's Hummer. We'll leave here at one in the morning. That should put us in the parking lot no later than two-thirty. They'll all be sleeping. Any questions?"

There were none, so I ended the meeting, told everyone to make their preparations, then get some rest. Me? I called Uber and went to the hospital where I spent an hour talking to Amanda. If she heard me, she gave no indication, so I went home, set the alarm for eleven o'clock and lay down on the bed. I hoped "to sleep, perchance to dream."

26

MONDAY, MAY 28, MIDNIGHT

I slept fitfully for maybe a couple of hours, and then I must have gone out like a light because the next thing I knew it was eleven o'clock and my iPhone was loudly playing "Don't Worry, Be Happy." *Oh yeah. That's what I'll do.*

I hauled myself off the bed and took a quick shower, dressed in black jeans, black tee, and black combat boots. I stood in front of the mirror and a me of more than three years ago stared dourly back. I hadn't dressed like that since I lost my brother Henry.

I checked my VP9, slid it into its holster on my right hip along with three extra mags; the body armor would have to wait until we arrived at our destination. It was way too bulky and heavy to travel in.

I went down to the basement where I found Bob, Tim, T.J. and his buddies ready and waiting for me.

"All is good?" I asked.

They all answered in the affirmative, except Tim.

"Tim?" I asked. "Are you okay? You sure you want to do this?"

"Yes, I'm sure. I was just going over my list, in my head, making sure I had everything. I do. I'm ready when you are."

I took a deep breath, nodded, and said, "Let's do it."

The drive to Marietta was uneventful and unusually quiet. I traveled with Bob in the Hummer along with the three amigos. Tim followed in his van.

We pulled into the strip mall parking lot at just after two o'clock that morning. All seemed quiet, but I felt decidedly uneasy when I looked around the lot. Our two vehicles were the only ones there, and I figured they'd attract the attention of the first police cruiser that happened by. That would be disastrous. How the hell we'd explain our presence, much less the arsenal we had inside the Hummer, I had no idea. No, it just wouldn't do. We couldn't afford to risk getting caught; we had to find another spot, and that posed our first setback. We had to find somewhere out of sight of the open streets, but it also had to be close to the warehouse.

"Drive around the block," I said to Bob.

He drove, we looked, and we saw nothing that even remotely looked like what we were looking for: a secluded spot within striking distance of the south end of the warehouse.

"Geez," I said. "This could be a deal breaker." Then I had a thought. "Go back to the mall, take the service road, and drive around the back."

At first I thought it was going to be a bust, that we'd have to take our chances and park in the lot, but then I spotted a large, yellow rental box van parked at the rear entrance to a furniture store which was adjacent to the rear entrance to a pizza restaurant—one of those all you can eat places. The pizza place was an end unit, and just a few yards beyond it and to one side was a large dumpster with just enough room to slide our two vehicles alongside. Provided no one looked too closely, they would be in the deep shadow of both the box van and the dumpster. The downside was that we were now more than a hundred yards from the warehouse security fence: most of it brightly lit open street.

This is not good, I thought. *We'll be exposed until we can get through the fence. If we get caught by the police— sheesh, I dunno. Well, I guess we'll just have to take our chances, and time's a wasting.*

"This will have to do," I said. "Park it, Bob."

He parked between the dumpster and the restaurant wall, and I exited the Hummer and went back to talk to Tim. He was already at work with his laptop.

"Harry," he said, obviously worried. "You can't do this from here. You'll be in full view of these two cameras. See, that one is covering the south end of the building." He pointed to the image on the screen. "And this one is covering the approaches from the street."

"Oh hell, now you tell me. You have access to them, right? Can you turn them off?"

"No. I told you. I can see what they see, but I can't control them. And even if I could turn them off, it would do you no good if they're being monitored—and you can bet that they are—it would set off every alarm in the place."

Damn it all to hell, I thought, furious with myself. *I should have thought of that.*

"So what the hell do we do, then?" I asked, more of myself than of Tim.

He thought for a minute, staring intently at the screen, flipping through the exterior from one to another, and then back again. He switched from the cameras to a satellite view of the building, studied it, then switched back to the cameras, flipped some more, then switched again to the satellite.

"There's a blind spot here, at the other end of the building." He pointed to the northeast corner. "As far as I can tell, there's no camera coverage between here and here. There's an open lot here, just across the street, behind the store. If you move the Hummer and park there, you'll be within thirty yards of the door at the south end, here. It's more exposed, but if you can get through the gate here, you'll be out of sight of the cameras and can access the building through this door here." He pointed to the rear entrance. "That door gives access to a passageway between the barrack rooms to the central vehicle storage area. The stairs to Christmas' living quarters are directly opposite. What do you think?"

I thought for a moment, then nodded, and said, "We don't have much choice, do we? What about you?"

"I can stay here. I won't launch until you tell me you're inside the fence. Make sure you're all in communication with each other and me."

I looked at him. "Tim, this is me. I'm not stupid."

He looked at me and grinned. "Just checking."

"What about the cameras inside? Can you pinpoint them for me?"

"Yup! There are two that you really need to watch out for, here and here. You'll have to take your chances, but if you move quickly, you can use the vehicles for cover. You'll be in view of either one of the cameras for just a second or two. If they're monitoring them, and they spot you, you're screwed. If they are just recording, you should be okay. Just keep your heads down—facial recognition has come a long way, so move fast."

I stared at him. "You're kidding, right?"

He shrugged. "No, sir, but it's two-thirty in the morning. I'd say they're all asleep."

"That's very reassuring, Tim. I'll be in touch," I said, slapped him on the shoulder and headed back to the Hummer.

It took a few minutes to explain the new plan, and then Bob drove around to the store at the northeast corner of the warehouse. It turned out to be an equipment rental store. Tim was right. How the hell we'd missed it the first go round I don't know. Probably because the frickin' alley to the side of the store was unlit, pitch black.

Bob eased the big vehicle down the alley and turned in behind the store. Perfect, we'd caught a break at last.

"Tim," I said, quietly. "Can you hear me?"

"I can. Check in please, everyone... Okay, comms are good. Are you in position?"

I told him we were, and he told me he was about to launch the drone.

"She's up, and I have you," Tim whispered a couple

of minutes later. "All five signatures and—oh Lordy," I heard Tim whisper. "I see twelve hot bodies. Eight of them are static, in the barrack rooms, so they must be sleeping, but four of them are moving; two at ground level traveling from north to south in the center aisle. They're on the east side of those vehicles, between them and the barrack room walls; must be guards."

"Where are the other two?" Bob asked.

"One is in a room on the west side, also on the ground floor, I think; the image is not quite so bright. Would that be the offices? If so, then he's probably monitoring the security system. The other is also on the west side, but his signature is much brighter, so he must be on the upper floor, above the office, south end, midway between the front entrance and the end of the building. I'd bet that's Christmas, and he's awake."

There was a moment of silence, and then Tim continued, "There are two sleepers in a room at the north corner of the entrance passage, three more in a room at the southeast corner of the building, and another three in the room next to them, that's the eight, plus the four on the move, that's twelve in all. Harry, I have fifty-one minutes of flight time left. Oh gosh, what was that? I think someone's coming. I gotta go. I'll be back soon, I hope."

"Oh hell," T.J. said. "That's not good. Now what?"

"We hope he's okay, and we do what we came to do," I said. "Load up. Vests, weapons, suppressors, balaclavas. And, grab some of those cable ties and duct tape; we're going to need them. Bob, grab the bolt-cutters and let's get moving."

We exited the vehicle and donned our gear. I slipped into the heavy tactical vest, checked the VP9 once more, more out of habit than necessity, slipped my tiny Sig and two extra mags into my vest pocket, and I too grabbed some of the cable ties, stuffed them in a vest pocket.

"Hey," Tim said in my ear. "It's okay. It was just a couple of stray dogs. They really scared me. I thought I was... Okay, never mind. I see you, but what are you doing? What's the plan?"

"Okay," I said, "here it is. Listen up, everybody. I want to keep this as clean as possible: no shooting unless you absolutely have to. I don't want this to turn into a damned bloodbath. The target is Nick Christmas; that's it. No one else gets hurt unless it's absolutely necessary."

I paused, waited for comments. There were none, just nods all around, so I continued.

"Bob, give me the bolt cutters. You guys stay here out of sight while I go open the gate. Then when I give the signal, you follow me. Once we're inside the compound, we go south staying tight against the wall to the rear entrance. No noise, *none!* I'll handle the door lock. Bob, you and I will take care of the two guards in the main storage area first, then the one in the office. Y'all got it?"

They had, so I continued, "Tim, it's going to be on you to keep an eye out for any unexpected movement, especially in the barrack rooms, and for God's sake keep an eye on Christmas."

"Yessir!" he replied. He sounded a little breathless and, on thinking about it, who could blame him?

"When we go in," I continued, "we'll stay out of sight

in the passageway. We wait until you give us the heads up, Tim, and then we subdue them.

"T.J.," I said, "you, Chuck and Monty will spread out and watch the barrack rooms. Anybody pokes their head out, you subdue 'em and strap 'em up. Don't shoot unless you absolutely have to. Above all, from the minute we leave this vehicle until we return, we keep our faces covered. If any one of us gets caught on camera, we're all screwed. Got it?"

They were excited, getting antsy, but they agreed.

"Okay," I continued. "We take the guy in the office down, and then we go for the stairs and find Christmas. Hopefully, we can take him by surprise."

"Question," Tim said.

"Go," I said.

"What do you intend to do with him when you get him?"

I looked at Bob. His face was a mask.

"Persuade him—"

"We're gonna dump him in that lake alongside Duvon James," Bob growled, interrupting me.

It wasn't exactly what I had in mind, and now that we'd reached the point of no return, I had serious doubts about terminating the man but... His stated intent was to kill August, and he'd already demonstrated that he fully intended to carry it through, so I really didn't have a choice.

"Oh," Tim said, "I see. You're going to... kill him?"

I ignored the question, and said, "Time to go. Cover your heads. Chuck, are you going to be able to keep up?"

He gave me a wry look. "Oh yeah!"

27

MONDAY, MAY 28, 2:30AM

Thirty-two Minutes

The padlock on the gate was a little tougher than I'd expected. The bolt cutters could have done with being a size bigger, but after a couple of attempts, the hasp finally gave with a crack that would have done credit to a .45 and left me breathing heavily. The thirty-five-year-old lock in the steel door wasn't the easy pick I'd thought it would be either. I must have fiddled with it for several minutes before Bob finally shoved me aside and grabbed the picks out of my hand.

"Oh, for God's sake," he growled. "Here, let me do it." I swear it took him less than thirty seconds. He shoved the door open and we slipped inside, into almost total darkness. The only light in the passageway leaked in indirectly from the central aisle. Chuck, the last man through the door, pulled it shut but didn't actually close it. We paused for a minute, listening. Somewhere, not far from where we were standing, I could hear footsteps and low voices talking together, and they were getting louder, closer.

"Tim," I whispered urgently. "Where are—"

"Maybe twenty-five feet and closing," he interrupted me.

"Move! Get out of the way," Bob said, ungently, shouldering me to the side. He moved silently, quickly, to the end of the passageway, stopped, and stood with his back against the wall, waiting.

They were both carrying automatic weapons. The instant the first guard appeared, Bob leaped forward, grabbed the barrel of his rifle, wrenched it out of hands, and in one sweeping movement, used it as a club to disarm the other guard.

They were taken completely by surprise, but they were well-trained and recovered in an instant, and they were good.

They'd obviously had advanced unarmed combat training because they attacked from both sides, knuckles advanced, kicking swinging, punching.

Bob, as big as he is, moved like a panther, crouched, dodging, ducking; they didn't land a single punch or kick, but he did. A single devastating knuckle punch to the throat and the first man went down on his knees, gasping for breath. The second backed off a little, composed himself, took two quick steps forward and... Bob sidestepped, turned slightly to his left, and landed a huge, roundhouse punch to the side of his head.

I was just about to leap into the fray, to go to his aid, when I suddenly realized he didn't need any help. I'd never really seen him in action before, other than the odd heavy-handed punch from which most mortals never got up. He was something to watch. He easily blocked every punch and kick, returning each with a devastating blow that carried his entire body weight. I'd studied Krav Maga, a little, but what Bob was doing was the real thing.

Krav Maga is a martial art first developed by the Israeli Defense Force to inflict as much pain and as quickly as possible on an attacker, often to the point of the attacker's death. Only once before had I seen it done better than Bob, and that was by Calaway Jones, who nearly ended my own life. It took a bullet to the head to stop her.

Anyway, that aside, it took Bob less than a minute to silently subdue the two guards. And another to strap them up and tape their mouths. *Now for the one on the west side,* I thought. *And then it's Christmas time.*

We found the guard in the office sitting behind a desk, his feet up, supposedly watching a bank of six security monitors, only he wasn't; he was playing a game on his phone.

"Hey," I said.

His surprise was complete.

"Are you winning?" I asked, pleasantly.

He didn't answer. I don't think he could. His jaw dropped, and so did his phone, and he sat frozen in his seat, staring at us, wide-eyed. Slowly, he raised his hand, more in protest than surrender.

"Now you just sit still and be a good boy," Bob said, stepping around the desk.

I held him at gunpoint while Bob did a number on him with cable ties and duct tape. We left him lying on the floor behind the desk, but before we did, I jerked all of the power cables out of the wall sockets. The monitors went black, the computers stopped humming, and it was suddenly so quiet the silence was... I know, I know, but I'm going to say it anyway: it was deafening.

Now, Nicky boy, I thought, grimly. *It's your turn.*

There was now no need to worry about the security cameras, so we quickly and silently climbed the stairs and, just as we reached the balcony, Tim shouted, "Look out behind you."

But it was too late.

"Hey, Bob, and Harry is it?" a soft voice said. "Yes, I thought so. Nice to see you both."

Shit! I thought, resignedly. *It's Christmas. Why am I not surprised?*

I glanced sideways at Bob. He was smiling.

"Now," Christmas said. "Please put your weapons on the floor, that's it; nice and gentle. Kick them away. Now your backups, nice and slow, please."

I reached behind me and slid the P938 out of its holster, placed it on the floor, and kicked it away. Bob did the same with his M&P9.

"Awesome," Christmas said, lightly. "And now put your hands in the air. Good, now turn around, and uncover your heads and drop the masks. You won't need them anymore. Good... slowly... keep 'em up, keep 'em up. That's it. All righty, then."

He was standing just inside an open door, a dark silhouette against the bright lights within the room, a Glock 17 in his right hand. He held it loosely, casually, pointed slightly downward. *My groin or Bob's?* I thought, grimly.

"Well, well," he said. "Who would have thunk it, except for me, of course?" He was smiling, but there was nothing friendly about it: lots of teeth and half-closed eyes that glinted blackly.

"Do come on in," he said, and casually waving the Glock from side to side, he backed slowly into what appeared to be a large private office. We did as he asked and followed him inside.

"I must say, Bob, after all these years I was beginning to wonder about you, but you've still got it. I had no idea you were here until just a few seconds ago. I'd offer you a job, but what use would you be to me? You'll be dead."

"Screw you, Nick," Bob said, seemingly without a care in the world. "I don't work for criminals... or creeps."

"No," Nick said, tilting his head slightly to one side, tapping the barrel of the Glock gently against the outside of his leg, "you always were a true company man, but they did let you go, right? Anyway, after that mess on the mountain, I had an idea you'd be coming after me. It's what I'd do, so I was kind of expecting you. And you almost made it, and would have if I'd been just a little more trusting. See, I don't trust anyone; never have, not even my closest friends, and certainly not the people that work for me. They're all... well, not nice people, shall we say? So, it was a little late when I found out you were here, in the building, but not too late... It's never too late, as they say, is it? Anyway, thanks to a little extra technology, I did get to know you were coming for me. Here, take a look."

Have you ever noticed how so-called smart people like to hear themselves talk? Nick Christmas was no exception. Without taking his eyes off either of us, he reached behind him and turned the laptop on the table around so we could see it. The image was frozen, but it showed a still shot of the two of us halfway up the stairs.

"Surprised?" he asked. "You shouldn't be, especially you, Bob, being CIA. You know," he continued, conversationally, "back in the day, when I was... oooh... ten years old, I think I was, I was a Boy Scout. That was quite a learning experience, as you can imagine, but the one thing I learned that has stayed with me ever since, that helped my career more than anything else, was the true meaning of the Boy Scout motto. Do you happen to know what that is? You, Harry. Do you know?"

Of course I did, but I wasn't about to give him the satisfaction of joining him in his game.

"Be prepared," he said, thoughtfully. "Be prepared, that's what it is, and I am, *always!*" The word snapped out of his mouth, then he smiled again, and slowly shook his head, watching me through slitted eyes.

"And I was," he said, pleasantly. "Fortunately, I was awake. And who wouldn't be after they'd just lost several million dollars' worth of equipment, not to mention sixteen of my assets... including poor old Hank, and Johnny, although Johnny... he was, well, I won't go into that. Anyway, I was working on my laptop, and up popped the warning flag. I had you from the second you put your foot on the stairs: motion detectors, you see, there at the foot of the stairs and here in my office. You set off the silent alarm and started the cameras rolling. One can't be too careful in this business. Now, please sit down; talk to me."

Neither of us moved to sit.

"Oh well, suit yourselves. I hope you don't mind if I sit." He sat down on the corner of the desk, his left foot on the floor, his right hanging loose, the gun held comfortably on his lap.

"So, Harry Starke," he said, smiling humorlessly at me. "You're something else—stand still, Bob," he snarled, interrupting himself, "or I'll shoot your frickin' dick off."

Bob didn't answer. Christmas turned his attention back to me.

"I dread to think how much money in manpower and equipment you've cost me these last couple of days. Oh no, Harry," he said as if he'd had a sudden thought. "My people downstairs. You killed them all, right?"

Neither of us answered.

He nodded. "Of course you did. It's what I would do," he said, for the second time. "So sad. Nice bunch of kids. 'Never mind. There are plenty more where they came from. But it's such a damned nuisance, you know, all that training down the shitter and now I have to start over."

He shook his head in mock exasperation, then said, "Harry, what the hell is it with you and your daddy? I offered to pay that family off, a really generous chunk of change, but he advised them to turn it down, said they'd do better in court. But, of course, I couldn't allow that, now could I? I couldn't let him drag me into court; who the hell knows what the old goat might uncover. And I did try to persuade him, but he wouldn't give an inch.

Now look where we are. He's about to lose a second son... and, well shit, it's all his fault. Where is he, by the way?"

He looked at me expectantly, then at Bob, then back at me and continued.

"Well, no problem. I'll find him. In the meantime, I need to deal with you guys."

We stared at him without speaking. My mind was churning. He was going to kill us both and, at that point, there was little I could do about it. The one advantage we had, if you could call it that, was we, Bob and I, were about ten feet apart. It would all depend on which one of us he went for first. I was betting it would be Bob.

"Okay," he said, twitching the barrel of the Glock, which was still lying in his lap. "As I see it, you guys are trespassing. You broke into my place of business, my home, and I caught you. You're both armed, and I'm in fear for my life so..."

We both saw it coming: the Glock began to rise and, just as he pulled the trigger, Bob dove to the left and I to the right, and even while I was in flight, I saw the puff as the bullet impacted Bob's vest.

I landed on my right side, rolling, reaching, scrambling for cover. I jerked the second Sig from my ankle holster as I rolled and snapped off two quick shots and I got lucky: the first shot missed and slammed into a photograph hanging on the wall; the second clipped his left hand ripping away his thumb. He howled with pain, staggered backward, the big Glock swinging in my direction as I continued rolling across the floor. And then I hit the wall and could roll no more. I jerked myself upright, my back against the wall. He disappeared behind the desk. I had no shot; Bob had no gun.

Me? I did something really stupid, something that, if it went wrong, if Bob didn't...

"*Bob!*" I yelled, and I flipped the Sig across the room to him. He reached up and snatched it out of the air.

I don't know if he saw me do it... I guess he couldn't have, but oh, he was quick, was Christmas, and he was good. His training took over. He stood up, flung himself to the left, shooting one-handed, aiming purely by instinct, thank God. If he'd taken his time and tried for a head shot, I'd be dead. But he didn't.

He managed to snap off two shots faster than you could blink. They slammed into my vest, center mass, less than two inches apart, just as he'd been trained to do.

Bob had also been trained that way. We all had, but Bob ignored his training. He waited, for just a split second, and went for the head.

The shot hit Christmas, whose attention was still on me, and the bullet entered his skull just forward of his right ear and angled slightly backward: the bullet ripped through his head and exited through his left ear and slammed into the wall, spraying blood, bone and brain matter across the room.

Bob collapsed, sat down on the floor with a thump, and lay there breathing heavily.

"Damn, that hurts," he said, softly, his hand on his vest just below his rib cage. "It feels like I've been kicked by a frickin' horse. That's three times in the last two days. Damn." He rolled over onto his side, facing me. "Hey," he said, worriedly. "Are you okay. You don't look so good. You hit?"

"Two to the chest. A horse, you say? More like being stomped on by an elephant."

"Yeah, right," he said, sarcastically, "a frickin' elephant. How the hell would you know?"

"Harry, Harry," I heard Tim in my ear. "What's happening? I heard shots."

"It's okay, Tim," I said. "Don't know about T.J. and the others, but we're both okay. Keep your eyes open for cops."

Bob turned and looked at what was left of Nick Christmas, shook his head, and said, "How do you like that, you sick son of a bitch. Payback for all of those women and children you defiled, and all of the poor bastards you murdered in Kandahar. Go rot in hell, where you belong."

I stared at him. *Where the hell did that come from?* I thought, but I wasn't about to find out, not then, at least.

"Well, Harry, old son," he said, lightly. "Problem solved, I guess, but we need to get outa here."

He groaned as he scrambled to his feet and offered me a hand up.

"Grab your mask and cover up," I said, wincing as the pain seared through my chest. "His troops downstairs must have heard the gunfire, and T.J. will—"

"I don't think so," Tim said, tentatively, into my ear. "I see eleven signatures, besides your own, and they're all bunched together in the center aisle across from the stairs where you are."

Bob grabbed Christmas' laptop, and we hurried out

onto the balcony and looked down. And there they were. All eight of them were lying face down, in a row on the floor, bound and gagged, with T.J., Chuck, and Monty standing over them. *What the hell? How did they manage that?*

"You said no noise, right?" T.J. said when I asked what the hell had happened, after we'd rejoined them. "So I figured—that is we figured, that there was no point in takin' any chances. If anyone of 'em had realized something was wrong, we'd have had a fight on our hands. We knew from Tim that they were all dead to the world, so we made a preemptive strike. Well, it was more a preemptive wakeup call than a strike. It was just a matter of rounding 'em up. So we went room-to-room, and we got 'em all; no fuss, no noise; problem solved. Better this way, right?"

"Yeah, right," I said, sarcastically. But I had to agree that he was right: it's always better to solve potential problems before they arise.

And so I took out my pocket knife, opened it, wiped it clean, closed it again and showed it to the nearest prisoner, then I laid it on a nearby table, told them to stay where they were and count to one hundred. We left the gang of eight lying there as we slipped away into the night. It was ten after three in the morning.

Thirty-two minutes, I thought. *Seemed like a frickin' lifetime.*

28

AFTERMATH

There's no describing the feelings I experienced that morning when I walked into August's home on Riverview and found him, Jacque, and Kate waiting for us. You'd be forgiven if you thought our reception was one of exuberance, but you'd be wrong. It was quite the opposite, in fact. Sure, they were relieved that we all made it home, for the most part unscathed, but after we'd told the tale, the stark reality of what we'd done over the past several days had descended upon us all like a giant wet blanket. There was nothing, nothing at all for us to rejoice about.

True, the threat to my father, Rose, and Amanda had been eliminated, but at what cost? And the repercussions? I didn't want to even think about what they might be. The reunion was somber, to say the least. Fortunately, it didn't last long. Such meetings can quickly deteriorate into maudlin gatherings of self-pity and doubt, and I wasn't about to let that happen.

So I sent Tim, Jacque, T.J., and his two buddies home.

Kate? As I said, she was there waiting for us, but she was hurting. The hearing loss in her right ear was almost complete. She'd stayed only to make sure we were all okay, and then she headed out to the emergency room to get treatment. I offered to go with her, but she would have none of it. For some reason, she wanted to be alone. Yeah, yeah, I know. She blamed me for it, and for the whole dang mess. I understood, and I sure as hell intended to make it right if I could.

The news, though, when it came later that same day, was good: Kate's right tympanic membrane was indeed ruptured, but the doctor had assured her it would heal naturally, by itself, in two or three months.

I forwent my usual nightcap of Laphroaig, not because I didn't want it, but because August didn't have any. Oh, he had some good scotch, but I had to be in the mood for that. I wasn't, so I settled for a steaming hot mug of Dark Italian Roast, which he did have, though not in the blend I... But I digress.

It was almost four-thirty that morning when I finally flopped down on the bed. Even so, I woke early, at around seven. It was after all, "the big day." If all went well, Amanda would wake up and... and? What? Would she blame me for what had happened to her? I wouldn't blame her if she did. And what about the baby... What if she didn't like the name I'd given her? So many questions, so many fears. There was nothing I could do until she woke up. *Hell, I'll just have to wait and see.*

So I rose from a deep sleep that morning, groggy and

with a head on me that felt like it was full of concrete. That, however, was not unusual. Usually, it's easily gotten rid of, a brisk five-mile run, and I feel like Rocky Balboa, on top of the world, but not that day. A run was out of the question: who the hell knew who I might encounter along the way? The press? Pitbull Charlie Grove? I couldn't and wouldn't face that, not yet.

So I settled for a long hot shower, and then I joined August in the kitchen.

"Good morning. What's the news?" I asked, nodding at the TV as I headed for the coffee machine.

"Not a word," he said over the rim of his cup. He was sitting at the kitchen table, his elbows on the tabletop, hands cradling the cup.

"You're kidding," I said.

He shook his head, and I sat down opposite him, and over the next ten minutes, drank two mugs of black coffee, ate a toasted onion bagel with cream cheese, and I felt like... I still felt like shit. And all the while I was watching the news. He was right. Nothing.

I checked the time. It was almost eight. I still had a couple of hours before I had to be at the hospital.

"Have you talked to Rose?"

"Yes, they're scheduled to land at nine-thirty. She'll bring Jade to the hospital. That okay?"

"Perfect," I said as I checked the TV for the umpteenth time. "I hope it won't be a wasted journey for them."

He looked sharply across the table at me. "I hear any more of that kind of talk, I'll slap you silly."

He wasn't joking, and I knew he wouldn't hesitate to

try, but somehow it struck me as being quite funny, and it lightened my mood, a little.

"Yeah, right," I said, smiling at him. "That'll be the day."

In the background, I could hear Charlie Grove speaking on Channel 7 and turned to watch. The guy was, as always, full of himself and his own importance, but he had a way with words, and he could grab your attention, but not that day. The local news was all minutia with a couple shootings thrown in for good measure, but not a word about last night's adventure.

"What do you think?" I asked, nodding toward the TV.

"Something isn't right," he said. "I checked every station before you came in, there's nothing."

I got up, filled my coffee mug for the third time and then sat down again. I picked up the remote and flipped through the channels, expecting to see... what? I really wasn't sure, but something, surely, about what had happened the night before, right?

Wrong!

Not a word, either about Marietta or Gypsum Pond, not on any of the TV channels, including those in Atlanta, of which Marietta is a bedroom community. And that I found to be extremely disquieting.

We continued watching until it was time to leave, at which point I reluctantly picked up the remote and turned the TV off.

"Time to go?" August asked.

"Yes," I said, taking a deep breath. I was nervous, I mean *really* nervous. My head was full of what-ifs: what if she doesn't come out of it? What if her brain's damaged? What if she's lost her memory and doesn't recognize me? What if... she hates me? *Geez, Harry. Get a frickin' grip. She'll be fine!*

"Yes," I repeated. "Let's go."

We arrived at the hospital at precisely ten o'clock. We stopped in at the flower shop, and I grabbed a huge bunch of, hell, I dunno, flowers—August bought an arrangement of daisies—and then we made our way through the maze of corridors to the waiting area just a few short steps from room 3007. There I left August to wait; this was something I had to do by myself.

I crept as quietly as I could to the door and peeked around the corner. She was lying there, eyes closed, breathing normally. I turned away and went to the desk.

"Where's Dr. Cartwright?" I asked.

"He's just getting out of surgery," the nurse said. "He shouldn't be too much longer. Is there anything I can do for you?"

I shook my head, disappointed. "Is it okay if I go and sit with my wife? She's in 3007."

At that, the nurse looked up and smiled. There was something about that smile...

"Of course. Go right ahead. I'll send in Dr. Cartwright as soon as he arrives."

And so I wandered back to her room, put the flowers on the nightstand, dragged a chair up to her bedside, sat down, took her hand gently in both of mine, and gazed at her face.

The bruises had lightened a little, the cuts on her lips were beginning to heal, her eyes were the most beautiful... shade... of... *Oh my God, they're open. She's awake.*

I couldn't speak. I sat there staring at her, transfixed, like I was some kind of loon.

"Hey," she said, and she gently squeezed my hand. It was barely a whisper, and hoarse, but it was the most beautiful sound I'd ever heard.

"Hey yourself," I finally managed to say. "Where the hell have you been?"

She smiled, just a little. "I can't talk, Harry."

"Oh... no, no, no, don't even try. I'll talk for both of us, okay?"

Again, she gifted me with that tiny, but oh so lovely smile. Oh my God, was I ever on cloud nine?

"The... baby?" she asked.

"She's fine. Absolutely fine. Beautiful. She's a she. I mean she's a girl. Gorgeous. She is, gorgeous. Just like you, well, not really, but she has your eyes, and that's what I called her, Jade. Is that okay? If it's not, we can change it. But her eyes are the same color as yours." I knew I was babbling, but I couldn't stop.

"She's with Rose. They're on their way. August is in the waiting area. They'll be here in a minute. Jade and Rose and August."

She was smiling up at me, her eyes watering, lips trembling, and I—

Dr. Cartwright walked in and saved me from making an even bigger fool of myself.

"Came out of it all by herself. Clever girl, aren't you, my dear? I took her off the drugs last night, had the nurses keep an eye on her. She came to at ten after three this morning, perky as can be. Well, not so much, and I had her kept under light sedation. But now that you're here, no more need for that, I think. So, my dear. How are we feeling?"

Ten after three, are you kidding me? That's exactly the time when we left the warehouse in Marietta.

She didn't even try to answer. She just looked up at him and rewarded him with the same tiny smile she gave me.

He nodded. "Right then. I'll leave you to it. Please don't excite her, and don't stay too long. The more rest she gets, the sooner she'll be out of here. Hello, who's this?"

I turned and saw Rose holding the baby, August behind them, all three smiling hugely. Well, no, Jade wasn't smiling at all. She was asleep.

"Can she?" Rose asked Dr. Cartwright.

"I don't see why not. Here, let me get out of the way."

He did, and Rose handed Jade to me, and I laid her down in the crook of Amanda's arm and stepped back. Jade stirred slightly in her sleep, opened her eyes, sighed, and then closed them again.

It was at that moment when I knew exactly what I was going to do with the rest of my life.

29

FOUR DAYS IN MAY

D r. Cartwright released Amanda the following Saturday morning, June 2. The five days following her awakening were hectic. The press finally found me at Riverview, and my world became a nightmare: I was obliged to face them head-on.

I gave Charlie Grove his exclusive, but I limited it to the attempt on Amanda's life and her improving condition. It wasn't exactly what he'd been expecting, but Channel 7's viewers certainly appreciated it.

That done, I held a press conference the following day, a one-time thing, I hoped, and answered questions for more than an hour about the foiled nuclear attack on the city. Some I could answer, some I was prohibited from answering, and some I just had no idea what the hell they were talking about, so I ignored them. Even so, I spent those next five days almost constantly dodging the reporters and cameras, but one thing I learned for certain was that the situation couldn't continue as it was.

Having dealt as best I could with the press, I figured

my next chore, if you can call it that, was to deal with Bob. No, I hadn't forgotten his perceived duplicity, nor would I until I had a full explanation. And so, early on Friday morning, the day before Amanda was due to come home, I headed downtown to my offices on Georgia Avenue.

Jacque, Tim, T.J., Bob and the rest of my team were more than a little enthusiastic in their welcoming me back. It was only then that I realized I hadn't been to the office and seen most of the team for more than three weeks. So, after thirty minutes of effusive conversation, I finally called a halt and asked Bob to join me in my office.

I had him take a seat opposite me, across the over-large coffee table that I used for less-than-formal meetings, and I put it to him.

"Bob," I said, quietly, "we have to talk. You know that, right?"

He'd been lounging comfortably in the corner of the sofa, but he sat up straight, narrowed his eyes, frowned and, for a minute, I thought he was going to get up and leave, but he didn't. He stared at me for a moment, then tilted his head to one side, looked away, and sighed.

"Okay, Harry," he said. "I guess you deserve some answers. Where would you like me to begin?"

I gave him a cockeyed look and said, "How about the beginning?"

He nodded, leaned forward, rested his elbows on his knees, and clasped his hands together in front of him and stared at them.

"I was twenty-two," he began, "academically gifted, so I was told, when I graduated college in 1993. I hadn't even left the campus when I was visited by—well, that I can't tell you. Let's just say this, as a result of that visit, I was recruited immediately into the CIA." He paused, looked up at me and smiled.

"Don't laugh, Harry," he said, "but I'd always been fascinated by James Bond and when the opportunity was offered... Ah, forget it." He shook his head and looked down at his hands.

"So anyway," he continued, "I spent my first year as a spook at Quantico before being transferred to the CIA's Office of Military Affairs; that was in '94. From then until I was 'deactivated' in 2005"—he made quotes with his fingers, then continued—"I was assigned to the Kabul Field office in Afghanistan where I had responsibility for coordinating CIA and DoD operational activities. When I was deactivated in 2005, after twelve years of service, I took a little time off and then spent the next two years as a cop in Chicago. I joined you in 2008, and that's it. The rest you know."

I stared hard at him and said, "Was coming here your idea or did someone put you up to it?"

He shook his head. "No, nothing like that. I hated being a cop, and I hated Chicago even more, especially the winters, so I came south. I needed a job. The PI thing fascinated me. So I did a little checking, found out that you were the best and, Bob's your uncle if you'll pardon the pun." He finally looked me right in the eye. "Look, Harry, I really am sorry. I should have been upfront with you, and I would have been if I could, but..." He shrugged. "I couldn't."

I nodded, slowly. I believed him. I had no reason

not to.

"And you're still part of the CIA? What exactly is your status?"

"That's something else I can't answer, not because of any regulation, but because I simply don't know. I'm still on the rolls, but I'm—as I told you—deactivated."

"So you could be *reactivated?*"

He shrugged. "I suppose, but why would they?"

If he didn't know the answer to that, I sure as hell didn't. So, still not really satisfied, or happy, I accepted the situation and left it at that. Other than firing his ass, I really had no other choice, and besides, there was something amiss about the way the events of those four days had been covered up.

I wanted answers to a whole boatload of questions. And I was hoping Bob could help get them.

Some, after much digging and hacking, we managed to get. Some, not even a sniff. Here's what we were able to find out:

As you know, there had been nothing in the media about the happenings in Marietta that night, not then nor any time since. And it was more than a week before we found out why. Actually, it was Tim who first found out; Bob confirmed Tim's findings at a later date.

It simply never happened.

Someone at the highest levels of the government, in all probability the NSA, had clamped down on and cleaned the building before the word leaked out. And when I say "cleaned," I think that was probably the understatement of the decade.

But that wasn't what bothered me—well, it bothered

me, but not to any great extent. We'd been careful, and I was certain they'd find nothing on the security system. I'd pulled the plug on that, remember? And we had the laptop. No, what bothered me was that someone had the power to erase that entire series of incidents, the whole four days, from reality, including the firefight on the mountain. That didn't make it to the media either, but even more scary was that they could effectively wipe away part of a man's existence. I'll explain that in a minute.

But going back to the warehouse: by six o'clock that morning, after we left, the word must have reached someone with decision-making authority, because a busload of—I'm going to say armed soldiers—arrived and locked the place down. By noon, the building was empty and abandoned. As I said, "cleaned."

What happened to Christmas' employees? We don't know. They disappeared, along with all of the vehicles, weapons, explosives, supplies, and every piece of paper and computer. Those assets already on assignment, including, so we think, Nick's girlfriend Jessica Roark, were quickly reassigned, absorbed, their identities changed.

Hank Johnson, we know, died during the fight on the mountain. What happened to the bodies, or Johnny Pascal, we never found out. Just as dawn was breaking that morning, several black helicopters were observed coming and going, to and from the site. What the sheriff found when he arrived later that afternoon, if he even bothered to respond to the call I made, I have no idea. He certainly didn't get in touch with me.

It was more than six months later when I returned to the cabin to find it gone, burned to the ground. Only the two stone chimneys and what once had been the basement remained to mark the spot. Fortunately, the cabin was insured.

Gypsum Pond? As you already know, Christmas cleaned that up himself.

Bob turned Nick Christmas' laptop over to Tim. Its contents were revealing, to say the least. Nick, so it seemed, had been a meticulous record keeper.

The women and children we'd discovered at Gypsum Pond were part of a slave and sex trafficking operation that Christmas and his crew had been running for almost a decade.

Lazarus, his Afghani partner, was never identified, but between them, over the years since Christmas had been discharged, they had imported more than seventy-four million dollars' worth of illegal drugs from Afghanistan, most of it heroin. His combined operations —not including his company's legitimate net earnings which were in excess of eighteen million dollars—Tim estimated to be more than one hundred million dollars, all of it missing without a trace.

I mentioned earlier that what bothered me most about the entire affair was that whoever was in charge of the cleanup operation had enough power to be able to effectively wipe away a man's life. I'll explain:

What happened to Christmas' body we never did find out. Bob, Tim, and I, we all tried to find out, through official channels—Tim, of course, went a little deeper than that—but as far as the government was concerned, he never existed. Well, not after 2008 when he was supposed to have been discharged. The official records stated that he died on August 25, 2008, while on active duty, the victim of an IED just outside of Kandahar, his body being cremated upon its return to the United States. We tried to reach his parents, but they had both passed several years earlier, and he had no siblings that we could find.

We, of course, knew different. The fact that more than ten years of his life had been completely expunged from the records as if he'd never existed, that really did bother me. And it raised a whole new set of questions the most pressing of which was... Why? Why was his slate wiped clean? Better yet: what was he really doing, and who for? Was it some obscure, clandestine government department? Or was it a breakaway faction of the DoD, Department of Defense, or some other covert, non-acronymic government agency operating to an agenda outside of and beyond its official mandate?

That, I think is the more likely answer. We always knew he'd been supplying security for the DoD, but I guess we'll never know.

Nick's laptop? It was dynamite, a ticking bomb. If it were ever to fall into the wrong hands, it would destroy us. I had Tim destroy it instead; problem solved.

But that still left me with more questions than answers, most of which would never be answered, including the most intriguing one of all: Who the hell had been pulling Nick Christmas' strings? I had no idea, but I knew damned well that whomever it was, he—maybe it was a she—sure as hell knew all about me.

30

FINALLY

I t was one of those balmy, late summer mornings in September. Amanda and I were lying side by side on loungers beside the pool. Jade was asleep in her stroller, and all seemed right with the world. It was the first time since Amanda had come home from the hospital that we were truly alone. The preceding three months had been hectic. We'd stayed at Riverview with August and Rose, until just two days earlier, that because Amanda had been pretty busted up and the healing was slow. Thus, she needed almost as much care and attention as did Jade.

Me? I was pretty damned useless and found it best to stay out of the way. What little time Amanda and I did have alone wasn't the time for talking, and the events leading up to her accident we'd never discussed, not until that morning and... Well, it was a long and very private conversation, most of which I'd rather keep to myself.

So, there we were, at our home on East Brow Road, enjoying the stunning view, the gentle rays, the warm breeze, and each other when suddenly she turned her head toward me and said, quietly, "I love you, Harry."

It wasn't so much what she said, more how she said it. Almost as a question.

"I love you too," I said cautiously.

She smiled and said, "But we need to talk."

"Oh-kay."

"That day, on the mountain, when Duvon ran me off the—"

"Amanda, hush," I said, interrupting her. "I'm so sorry..."

"No, please, don't be." She rose up on her elbow and turned toward me. "It was my fault. I was angry with you. I thought the round trip would take too long. I was within days of giving birth. Harry, I could have killed Jade."

"But you didn't." I also raised myself up and turned to face her. "And it wasn't your fault. Look, it's over. Duvon is gone, so's Shady. But you're right. We do need to talk, but not about that. Look, all this... this... stuff that's gone down, this crazy cycle of violence; it has to end. We have to get past it, move on, make a proper life for ourselves... for the three of us."

I sat up, swung my legs off the lounger, and turned to face her. I took her hand in mine and looked deep into her eyes. Some of the scars hadn't yet quite faded, some would always remain, but to me, she was more beautiful than ever.

"It's over," I said, quietly. "I'm going to resign, give up my half of the business—"

"You can't," she said, pulling her hand away. She stood up, folded her arms, lowered her head, and walked a small circle on the concrete patio. Then she stopped, looked at me, sat down again, face to face, and said, "Harry, you can't do that. I won't let you."

I smiled at her, took both her hands in mine, raised them to my lips, kissed her knuckles, then looked up at her and shook my head.

"What happened to you, my love, was to have been the final straw for my career as a private eye. But then Joe was kidnapped. I don't want to talk about it, but that really was the end, for me at least."

I was, of course, referring to the Christmas fiasco.

She twisted her hands out of mine and said, "Okay. Let's think about it. You're done, finished, no more Harry Starke Investigations. Now what? What are you going to do for the next forty years?"

Forty years? That's a bit optimistic.

"Enjoy life. You, Jade, more kids?" I said with a smirk.

"And just how long do you think it would be before you became bored with all that *enjoyment?*"

She tilted her head, narrowed her eyes, and looked into mine. "Come on. Tell me. How long?"

She had me there. Hell, my attention span for the mundane was that of a lemon.

"And there's another thing," she said, "several in fact." She grabbed my hands. "Harry, where do you think we'd be today if you weren't you? If you didn't do what you do so well? If you'd been off somewhere *enjoying life?* No, don't answer. I'll tell you." She turned and looked out over the patio wall at the city laid out below and nodded.

"All of that would be gone, Harry, and thousands of

lives along with it, including all of your family and friends. This view that you, that we, love so much would be nothing but a nuclear wasteland. It's still there because you were doing what you do best, Harry.

As I followed her gaze, I was speechless. Such thoughts had never entered my head.

"But I'm not—"

"A hero? Yes, you are, and no buts. You know I'm right. This is your town, and mine, and now Jade's and all those other kids you'd like to have. Now shut the hell up and come kiss me."

I did. I shut up, and I kissed her. And then I had another thought: *How come she always gets the last word?*

At that very same moment, more than fourteen hundred miles away, on a beach on the eastern shores of the Dominican Republic, Lester "Shady" Tree, known locally as Sam Cooper, was enjoying a tall glass of iced rum and cola. He was in paradise, not wanting for anything. Life was good, except... *Harry Frickin' Starke!* he thought, savagely.

AUTHOR'S NOTE:

This is the 14th novel in the Harry Starke series, and is the follow up to Apocalypse. I hope you enjoyed it. If you did enjoy the story, please consider posting a short review on Amazon. Will there be more Harry Starke stories? Yes, of course. In fact, I'll have several surprises for in the coming months

Oh, and one more thing: if you'd like to stay up to date with news about Harry, Amanda, Kate, and the rest of the characters yes, there's lots more to come - you can click here to sign up for my bi-weekly newsletter. And, for you paperback aficionados, here's the full URL: https://www.subscribepage.com/blairsnewsletter.

CPSIA information can be obtained
at www.ICGtesting.com
Printed in the USA
FSHW021337020621
82025FS